THE HALF-BREED
"Witty, tender, strong characters and plenty of action, as well as superb storytelling, make this a keeper."

BRIDES OF DURANGO: JENNY
"Bobbi Smith has another winner. This third installment is warm and tender as only Ms. Smith can do . . . Fans will not be disappointed."

BRIDES OF DURANGO: TESSA
"Another wonderful read by consummate storyteller Bobbi Smith . . . Filled with adventure and romance, more than one couple winds up happily-ever-after in this gem."

BRIDES OF DURANGO: ELISE
"There's plenty of action, danger and heated romance as the pages fly by. This is exactly what fans expect from Bobbi Smith."

HALF-BREED'S LADY
"A fast-paced, frying-pan-into-the-fire adventure that runs the gamut of emotions, from laughter to tears. A must-read for Ms. Smith's fans, and a definite keeper."

OUTLAW'S LADY
"Bobbi Smith is an author of many talents; one of them being able to weave more than one story . . . Ms. Smith creates characters that one will remember for some time to come."

THE LADY & THE TEXAN
"An action-packed read with roller-coaster adventures that keep you turning the pages. *The Lady & the Texan* is just plain enjoyable."

RENEGADE'S LADY
"A wonderfully delicious 'Perils of Pauline' style romance. With dashes of humor, passion, adventure and romance, Ms. Smith creates another winner . . ."

"STOP RIGHT NOW!"

He commanded. "Jackson and his men had the ambush all planned out. They knew exactly what they were doing. You took a head shot. You're lucky to still be alive, outgunned the way you were."

"I don't think so." In her heart, Dusty felt as if a part of her had already died. Only her driving hatred for Jackson and his men gave her the inner strength she needed to keep going. "My father should never have been killed! He and Matt were good men. They'd never hurt anybody. Those outlaws murdered them both—and for what? Money? Jackson and his men think money is more important than people's lives?"

"There are bad people in this world. That's why I became a Ranger. I want to stop as many of them as I can, and I'm going to stop Jackson and his men—real soon."

"And I'm going to help you," she said fiercely.

"No, you're not," he stated.

She glared at him as she told him, "But I heard Jackson and his men talking, and I know where they're going."

"Where?"

She was defiant as she met his challenging gaze. "I won't tell you—not unless you agree to take me along."

Other books by Bobbi Smith:

RUNAWAY
WANTED: THE TEXAN
RAPTURE'S TEMPEST
WANTED: THE HALF-BREED
LAWLESS, TEXAS
HIRED GUN
DEFIANT
HALFBREED WARRIOR
BRAZEN
BAYOU BRIDE
HUNTER'S MOON (HALF MOON RANCH)
FOREVER AUTUMN
LONE WARRIOR
EDEN
WANTON SPLENDOR
SWEET SILKEN BONDAGE
THE HALF-BREED (SECRET FIRES)
WESTON'S LADY
HALF-BREED'S LADY
OUTLAW'S LADY
FORBIDDEN FIRES
RAPTURE'S RAGE
THE LADY & THE TEXAN
RENEGADE'S LADY
THE LADY'S HAND
LADY DECEPTION

The Brides of Durango series:

ELISE
TESSA
JENNY

Writing as Julie Marshall:

MIRACLES
HAVEN

Bobbi Smith

Relentless

LEISURE BOOKS NEW YORK CITY

This book is dedicated to my first granddaughter!
The perfect Willow Marie!

A LEISURE BOOK®

March 2010

Published by

Dorchester Publishing Co., Inc.
200 Madison Avenue
New York, NY 10016

ISBN 10: 0-8439-6282-8
ISBN 13: 978-0-8439-6282-6
E-ISBN: 978-1-4285-0818-7

Visit us on the web at www.dorchesterpub.com.

Relentless

Prologue

It was a hot late-summer night. Fifteen-year-old Grant Spencer was with his father, the sheriff of Grand Bluff, when one of the men from town came running into the office.

"Sheriff Spencer! You gotta get down to the saloon! They need your help. There's some serious trouble brewing," Will Collins warned.

"What's wrong?" Dan Spencer saw Will's desperation and immediately stood up and came around his desk. It was Saturday night on a payday weekend, so he'd been expecting a ruckus. It wasn't unusual for the local ranch hands to come into town and get a little wild, but Will sounded as if there was more to this trouble than just drunken cowboys.

"It's Al Reynolds. He's full of whiskey and threatening to shoot up the place!"

Dan was worried as he started to leave the office. Al Reynolds was a real troublemaker when he was sober, and he only got worse when he was drinking. Dan paused just long enough to tell his son, "Stay here."

"But I can help you—" Grant offered.

Dan understood the boy's desire to go along, but he also knew just how dangerous the saloon might get and he wanted Grant safe.

"Not tonight. Stay here at the office." It was an order. There were times when he did take Grant along on his rounds, but if Reynolds was as drunk and as dangerous as Will said, the saloon was no place for his son.

Dan strode from the office with Will Collins hurrying along behind.

Young Grant felt uneasy as he watched them go. Will wasn't the bravest of men, and Grant knew he would be of little help to his father if the brawl turned ugly. He was worried about his father facing the drunk Al Reynolds all alone. Not that his father couldn't handle Al. He could. His father was a fine lawman, and he'd kept Grand Bluff peaceful for a long time now. But from the way Will had been acting, there was no telling what was really going on at the saloon tonight.

Grant wanted to go after them. He wanted to grab a shotgun from the gun case and back his father up, but he also knew how angry his father would be if he did not obey his order to stay behind. Reluctantly, he went to stand by the office door to await his father's return.

Dan could hear the raucous noise of the fighting coming from the saloon as he drew near, and he knew this situation wasn't going to be easy to control. He stopped long enough to speak to Will. "You got a gun on you?"

"No," the frightened man answered.

"Then get out of sight."

Will quickly ran off to hide in the darkened nearby alleyway.

There had been a few times over the years when Dan had wished he'd had a deputy working with him. Judging from the sound of things, tonight was one of those nights. But no matter what, he was the sheriff and he would handle the problem.

Just as Dan neared the front of the saloon, Al Reynolds came flying out of the swinging doors and tumbled heavily into the street. Tom Lawson, one of the hands from a nearby ranch, stepped outside the saloon and stood there, laughing at the drunk where he lay sprawled in the dirt.

"Had enough for one night, Reynolds?" Lawson sneered.

"No! Have you?" In a mindless rage, Al struggled to his feet.

"I've had all I want of you." Lawson turned to go back inside. "I got some more drinking to do."

"But I'm not done with you!" Humiliated and furious, Al drew his gun and fired at the other man.

Even as drunk as he was, at this close range his aim proved true. Lawson collapsed and lay unmoving.

At the sound of gunfire, screams erupted from inside the saloon. The saloon girls and their customers rushed to the swinging doors to see what was going on just as Dan confronted the drunk.

"Drop the gun, Reynolds!" Dan shouted, going for his own revolver.

But Al Reynolds wasn't taking orders from anybody. Before Dan could even clear his gun from his holster, Reynolds turned on him and fired. Dan collapsed and lay unmoving in the dusty street.

As Reynolds stood there, staring at the dying sheriff, the realization of what he'd done slowly sank in and he panicked.

"Get back! All of you!" He fired a few wild shots in the direction of the saloon and then ran off into the night. He knew he had to get out of town and fast.

Those in the saloon ran for cover.

Having seen Reynolds take off, Will came out from where he'd been hiding in the alley watching, and knelt down beside the fallen sheriff.

"Sheriff— How are you?" Will could tell the other man had been gut-shot and he was bleeding profusely.

Dan was dying and he knew it. "My boy—" he managed in a pain-ravaged voice. "Get my boy—"

"I need help!" Will called out in desperation. "Somebody get the doc!"

Those inside the saloon were starting to venture back outside to see what had happened. They were horrified by the scene before them. One man ran for the doctor while several others checked on Lawson, only to find he was already dead. Hal, the bartender, came rushing over to Will and the sheriff.

"Go get Grant. He's down at the sheriff's office," Will said.

Hal only needed one quick look at the severity

of the lawman's wound to understand why Dan wanted his son. He hurried off to get the boy.

It wasn't long before Doc Murray was there, kneeling beside Dan. He took one look at his gunshot wound and quickly directed the men standing around. "We need to get him over to my office. Now!"

The men all pitched in to help. One got a buckboard, and they quickly lifted Dan into the back of it to transport him down the street to the doctor's office.

Grant had been waiting nervously for his father's return. He'd grown even more worried when he'd heard several gunshots being fired and then complete silence. He'd almost been ready to get the shotgun out of the gun case and go after his father when he saw Hal running up the street toward him. Grant ran from the office to meet him.

"What is it? Where's my father?" Grant demanded as he met the bartender in the street.

"He's been shot, Grant. They're taking him over to Doc Murray's place—"

Grant didn't say another word; he just took off. They had just finished carrying his father into the office when he got there. Grant rushed inside to find the other men about to leave and Dr. Murray hard at work cutting away his father's shirt to examine the wound. He looked up to see the boy coming in.

"Pa—" Grant couldn't hold back the cry that tore from him.

Dan was bleeding heavily, in spite of the doctor's best efforts to stop the blood loss. He was barely conscious, but at the sound of Grant's voice, he opened his eyes and lifted his hand to him. "Grant—"

Grant was beside him in an instant, grabbing his father's hand as he gazed down at him. "I'm here, Pa— I'm here—"

The wound was grievous, and Dr. Murray knew there was nothing he could do to save his patient. He backed away to give father and son privacy for what little time Dan had left.

Dan looked up at his boy. "I love you, son," he managed.

"I love you, too—" Grant said in an emotion-choked voice. "You'll be all right. Dr. Murray will get the bullet out. It'll be—"

"No, Grant—" Dan drew on the last of his strength. "Grant— I—"

His eyes closed as his life slipped away from him.

"Pa!" Grant grew frantic as he looked helplessly to the doctor. "Doc— Do something! You have to do something—"

Dr. Murray knew there was nothing more to be done. "I'm sorry, Grant—"

"No!"

He left Grant alone with his father to grieve. As he went outside, he saw that many of the men were still there, waiting to hear how the sheriff was doing, so he went outside to talk to them.

"He didn't make it, boys," he told them grimly.

"Who did this? Who shot Sheriff Spencer and Lawson?"

"It was Al Reynolds!" one man shouted.

"Where is he? Where did he go?" the doctor demanded, wanting to see justice done. Dan Spencer had been a good man and a fine father. He hadn't deserved to be shot down in cold blood by a drunken fool.

"He ran off," Will put in.

"Then you'd better get a posse together and find him. That man's a murderer," he said angrily.

"The doc's right! Let's start searching for him. As drunk as he was, he might still be in town!" Hal said.

They spread out to begin the hunt for the killer.

Dr. Murray waited for Grant to come out of the office. He could see how the youth was suffering and wanted to help him in any way he could.

"The men from town are out looking for Al Reynolds."

"He's the one who shot my father—"

"Yes."

"If they don't find him, I will," Grant said fiercely.

"Your father was a fine man."

"I know." Grant fell silent, unable to say any more.

"Let's go inside," Dr. Murray encouraged, taking the boy into a small sitting room where they could be alone and talk.

Grant stayed with the doctor until Hal and the other men returned to speak with them.

"Did you find him?" Grant asked, coming to his feet to face the men from town.

"No. One of the boys down by the stable said they saw him ride out right after all the shooting. We're going to go after him at first light," Hal promised.

Grant's expression was iron-willed and fierce as he looked at the bartender who'd been his father's friend. "I'm riding with you."

Sadly, Hal regarded the boy who had just been forced to become a man. "I figured you would. We're meeting at the stable at five."

"I'll be there."

Hal looked to the doc. "Can we help in any way?"

"Yes. Before you ride out, we'll see Dan put to rest."

Grant looked over at the doctor. He remembered the sorrow that had come when they'd buried his mother six years before and he knew how hard this was going to be. "We can bury him next to my mother."

"Yes, we'll do that," Dr. Murray assured him.

Grant went back inside to say his final good-bye to his father. After a time, Dr. Murray went to speak with Grant, and when Grant was ready to leave, Hal was still there waiting for him.

"I'll be staying the night with you," Hal said. The boy was carrying his father's gun belt and the personal things the sheriff had had on him.

"Thanks—" Grant's voice was tight with emotion as they headed across town to the sheriff's office, where he and his father lived in two back rooms.

When they went in, Hal asked, "Do you need anything?"

Grant wanted to say "my father back," but he didn't. "No, but Hal—"

"What?"

"I'm sure Pa would have wanted you to have this—" Grant handed him his father's sheriff's badge.

Hal stared down at it in deep sorrow, and yet he was honored by the gesture. He looked Grant in the eye as he pinned it on his shirt. "I'm gonna make him proud of me, boy."

Grant got no sleep that night. He lay in bed, staring off into the darkness, wondering what the future held for him. Near-violent emotions tormented him. He was torn between rage and sorrow. He longed for the comfort of his father's nearness. He had always felt safe when his father was with him, and he realized now, he would never know that feeling again. There were cruel, vicious men like Al Reynolds out there, and they had to be brought to justice. They had to be made to pay for their evil deeds.

Hal had bedded down in one of the jail cells, and he was up before dawn. He wasn't surprised to find Grant dressed, ready to ride, and wearing his father's gun belt. Little was said as they headed down to the stable to meet the other men who would ride with them. The posse galloped out of town, determined to track down the killer.

It wasn't easy. Al Reynolds had gotten a good head start on them, but they stayed on his trail for days on end. There were times when some of the men in the posse thought about giving up and going home, but Grant's fierce determination to bring his father's killer to justice kept them going.

And their persistence ultimately paid off.

They finally caught up with Reynolds in a small canyon where he was camped out.

Reynolds was relaxing beside his campfire, drinking some whiskey and getting ready to bed down for the night. He thought he'd made a great escape. He thought he'd gotten clean away from Grand Bluff. He thought he would never have to pay for killing the sheriff and Lawson. He was right in the middle of taking a deep swallow when a voice he recognized all too clearly as Hal's came to him out of the darkness.

"Don't even think about trying to make a run for it, Reynolds. We got you covered on all sides," the bartender called.

"Hal?" he blurted out in shock.

"That's right," Hal said slowly as he stepped out into the light of the campfire along with several other men.

Reynolds couldn't believe Hal, the bartender, was wearing the sheriff's badge or that Dan Spencer's son was with them and carrying a gun that he had pointed straight at Al's heart.

"We're taking you in," Hal stated firmly.

Reynolds knew he'd rather die now than hang later. He started to go for his gun, but Grant was ready for him.

Grant got off a shot that hit him in his gun arm and left him writhing on the ground in pain.

"Good shot, Grant. Go on, now. Finish him off," one of the other men in the posse urged. He hated what Reynolds had done and wanted to see him pay for his murderous ways.

Reynolds looked up at the sheriff's son standing over him, his gun still aimed straight at him, and he knew true terror.

It would have been easy for Grant to pull the trigger, but he didn't. "No. I'll let the law decide his punishment," he said. "You're going back to stand trial, Reynolds."

The other men in the posse were impressed by Grant's self-control and determination as they quickly tied up the moaning killer. They bound his wound and then waited for daylight to start back home. The hunt was over. They'd gotten their man.

One Month Later

Grant stood over his father's grave, staring down at the small cross that marked his final resting place. Reynolds had been convicted in his trial and had hanged that morning. Grant had thought he would be at peace now, but the killer's death hadn't brought his father back. He was still alone.

"Grant—" Reverend Williams had seen young Spencer come up to the cemetery and had followed him there to see if he could help in any way. "Are you all right? Can I do anything for you?"

"No."

"You're welcome to come live with me and my wife if you'd like."

Grant turned away from his father's grave to talk to the reverend. "I appreciate it, but Tom Grady's offered me a job on his ranch, and I told him I'd take it—for now."

"For now?"

Grant looked up at the preacher. As their gazes met, Reverend Williams could see the fierce determination in the hardness of the young man's expression.

"That's right." Grant had done a lot of thinking in the last few days, and he'd decided the best way he could honor his father was to become a lawman, too. "I'm going to work for Tom until I'm old enough to pin on a badge."

Chapter One

Canyon Springs, Texas
Ten Years Later

Stagecoach driver Charley Martin was feeling good as he reined in the team of horses in front of the small stage office in town. After his six-day run, he was finally home, and it felt good. He was looking forward to spending time with his wife, Mary Anne, and daughter, Justine—or Dusty as he liked to call her.

Charley smiled as he thought of Dusty. She was getting older now—she was already seventeen—but her childhood nickname still fit. She'd had trouble saying her name when she was little. Her pronunciation of Justine had come out closer to Dusty, and because she loved being outside and helping him whenever she could, the nickname fit. She wasn't afraid of a challenge, and, having seen the spirit in her early, he'd taught her how to ride astride and use a gun. Their town could be a wild place, and there was no telling what might happen. With his being on the road so much, he wanted Dusty to be able to defend herself and her mother. He'd been missing them and couldn't wait to have a home-cooked meal and sleep in a comfortable bed tonight.

Hank Jones, the clerk in the stage office, had been nervous as he'd kept watch for the stage all afternoon. He'd known Charley was due back in today and the news he had for him was bad. When he saw his friend drive up, he went outside to talk to him, knowing it was going to be one of the most difficult conversations he'd ever had in his life.

Charley had just finished tossing the luggage down to the two men who had been his passengers on the trip when he saw Hank come outside.

"Hey, Hank— We made good time, considering the storm we ran into," Charley said as he climbed down to speak with his friend.

"It's good you're back. Come inside for a minute," Hank said.

Charley glanced down the street, eager to head for home, but he knew business came first. He followed his friend into the office and was rather surprised when Hank waited at the door and then closed it behind them. He tensed, knowing something wasn't right. "What is it?"

"You want to sit down?"

His expression hardened. "Hell, no. What's going on?"

"It's bad news, Charley—" Hank looked him straight in the eye as he said, "It's Mary Anne— I'm sorry—"

"Sorry? What are you sorry about? What about Mary Anne?" Confusion overtook him. He couldn't imagine what Hank was talking about.

"It was a bad fever— Came on real suddenlike— She died three days ago—"

Charley could only stare at him in disbelief. *Mary Anne, dead?* He couldn't believe what he was hearing. Numb and confused, he immediately thought of his daughter. "Where's Dusty?"

"The Randolphs took her in—"

Charley was thankful for the Randolphs. Fred Randolph owned the local general store and was a good friend. He was out the door before Hank could say any more.

Dusty was in the kitchen at the Randolph house with her friend Francie and Mrs. Randolph, helping to prepare dinner, when they heard the loud knock on the front door. She looked at Francie anxiously.

"It might be my father—" She knew he was due back in town that afternoon if he'd been able to stay on schedule, and she desperately needed to be with him.

Francie gave her a quick hug and then they followed her mother into the front hall. Mrs. Randolph had just answered the door and in that moment Dusty saw her father standing on the front porch. A tormented cry escaped her as she rushed to him.

"Oh, Papa—" Heartbroken, she went into his arms, finally giving vent to the grief she'd tried to control these past days.

Charley held her close as he looked up at Mrs. Randolph, all the pain he was feeling revealed in his eyes. "Thank you for taking Dusty in."

Mrs. Randolph touched his arm sympathetically. She had known this moment would come and realized father and daughter needed their privacy to come to grips with what had happened.

"Why don't you and Dusty go on into the parlor?" she offered. "Francie and I will be in the kitchen if you need us—"

She drew Francie away with her, leaving them alone.

Charley and Dusty moved into the sitting room and sat down on the sofa.

A torrent of emotions filled Charley as he faced his future. He still couldn't believe it—

Mary Anne was—dead.

The pain of losing his beloved wife was like a knife in his soul. He had no idea what he was going to do without her. She had meant the world to him—and now— Again, thoughts of his loss overwhelmed him.

Dusty clung to her father, taking solace in his loving embrace. She knew their lives had been changed forever, but they still had each other.

When they finally left the Randolphs' house some time later, Dusty took her father to visit her mother's grave in the small cemetery behind the church. The sight of the simple white headstone and freshly turned earth brought new tears. It was a long time before they returned home.

Much later, Dusty lay alone in her bedroom unable to sleep. She wondered what was going to happen next. Her father was due to leave town again on his next run in just two days. She wanted to stay with him. She loved him. He was all she had left. Sleep was a long time coming for her that night.

* * *

Charley sat alone in the kitchen in the wee hours of the morning, staring down at the half-empty bottle of whiskey sitting before him on the table. He couldn't go upstairs and sleep in the bedroom where his beloved wife had died. He would rather pass out there at the table. He'd been trying to drown his sorrow in the potent liquor, but had found little release in his drunkenness. If anything, the liquor made him feel even worse. Disgusted, he pushed the bottle across the table away from him.

Charley frowned, wondering what the future was going to bring. His daughter was an innocent. She was too young to be left there at the house all alone while he made his runs, and they had no other family nearby. Slowly, he came to realize the only way he could keep Dusty safe was to take her with him. He didn't know how she'd take to the idea, but there was nothing else he could do.

His decision made, he pushed away from the table and got up to stagger into the parlor, to try to get some sleep on the sofa. In the morning, he would tell Dusty what he had decided. He only hoped she would be content with his decision. From now on, she would be riding shotgun with him on the stage.

Dusty got up early the next morning and went downstairs to find her father asleep on the sofa. She was quiet as she went out into the kitchen. She found the whiskey bottle on the table and quickly put it away before starting to cook breakfast for him. She was busy frying the bacon and eggs and making biscuits when her father appeared in the doorway. He had been and always would be her hero, and she went to give him a kiss on the cheek.

"Good morning. I thought you might like some breakfast," she offered, going back to her cooking.

"I appreciate it," he said in a gruff voice as he went to sit at the table. His head was pounding, and he knew he wouldn't be drinking again anytime soon. "We need to talk."

Dusty looked over at him from where she was standing by the stove. "I know. What are we going to do?" The uncertainty of life without her mother was frightening to her. It had all happened so fast. There were still moments when she expected to see her mother walking into the room or to find her sitting in her favorite chair in the parlor doing her needlework.

"Well, from what I can figure, there's only one thing we can do—" Charley looked up at her.

She waited in silence for him to continue.

"I know this may be hard for you—"

An unexpected sense of agony filled her as she feared he might be planning to send her away somewhere—to a boarding school or possibly some unfamiliar relative back East.

"But I want you to start going with me on my stage runs."

"What?" She was shocked and relieved at the same time to know they would be staying together.

"I can't leave you here by yourself, so the only thing we can do is have you ride with me." His gaze met hers across the room. "I thought we could get you some other clothes. If we cut your hair and you dress like a boy, none of the passengers would suspect you're a girl, especially with a name like Dusty You could ride shotgun. I know you'll be giving up a lot, but I have to know you're safe, and that's the only way."

Charley was unsure how she was going to react. He was watching her carefully now, trying to judge her reaction.

Dusty was shocked—

Cut her hair?

And wear boys' clothes?

She was momentarily confused and then realized her father was right. The disguise could work. She would make sure of it. Her whole life was going to change, but she didn't care. She and her father only had each other now, and they needed to be together. She looked at him, tears shining in her eyes. "I want to be with you, Papa. That's all that matters."

Hugely relieved, he managed a melancholy smile as he got up to go and hug her.

"We'll buy the clothes today, so you can start getting ready."

It was late in the afternoon on the following day when Francie arrived at the house to see Dusty.

"I'm glad you could come over," Dusty told her friend as she let her in. "I need your help."

"Of course, what can I help you with?" They hadn't talked since Dusty had returned home with her father.

Dusty quickly explained how she was going to

be traveling with her father when he left town the following day.

"So you're just going to be riding along in the stage with the passengers while he's driving?"

"It's a little more complicated than that—"

"What do you mean? I don't understand."

"Well—" She paused for a moment, knowing her friend was going to be shocked. "Actually, when we leave, I'm going to be riding shotgun for him—"

"You're what?" Francie could only stare at her.

"I want to stay with my father, so he said I could ride shotgun with him, but to do that—"

"What are you talking about?" She was still trying to accept the surprising announcement.

Dusty met her friend's gaze straight on. "With my mother gone, this is the only way I can stay with Papa, but to do that I need your help. Come on into my room with me."

She grabbed Francie by the hand and drew her down the hall to her small bedroom, shutting the door behind them.

"Here." Dusty handed her a pair of scissors.

"You want me to cut your hair?"

"Yes—real short. If I'm going to do this, I have to look like a boy."

Francie looked from the scissors to her friend's beautiful, long, thick mane of dark hair. "You're sure about this?"

Dusty looked at Francie, her expression serious. "Yes. I'm sure."

"All right."

True friend that she was, Francie set to work.

Half an hour later, Francie was waiting in the parlor when Dusty appeared in the doorway.

"Well, take a look. What do you think?" Dusty asked. She had changed into the boys' clothes her father had bought her and was as ready as she would ever be to start her new life.

Francie spun around to face her friend and was amazed by the complete change in her appearance. Standing there before her clad in loose-fitting pants, a work shirt, boots and hat was someone who appeared to be a young boy of maybe fifteen or sixteen.

"I can't believe it—"

"I really look like a boy?"

"Oh, yes." Francie doubted anyone in town would recognize Dusty at first glance. "This disguise is going to work."

Dusty grinned. "Good. Papa will be glad. This will make things a lot easier for us."

"Are you comfortable?" Francie knew Dusty had had to tightly bind her breasts with a length of cloth to disguise her figure.

"I'll get used to it. I have to." She twisted and shrugged a little, testing the binding.

Francie went to her and gave her a quick, reassuring hug. "I'm going to miss you while you're gone."

"I'm going to miss you, too, but I'm trying to look at this as a big adventure. I've always wondered what Papa did on his trips, and now I'm going to find out."

"Just be careful."

"I will be."

They visited for a little while longer and then

Francie had to go home. She gave Dusty one last hug, knowing her friend was going to have a lot of wild stories to tell her when she got back to town after this first trip.

Charley returned home a short time after Francie had left. He'd been down at the stage office making sure everything was set for them to leave first thing in the morning. When Dusty met him in the hallway, his first look at his daughter left him grinning broadly.

"I'd say you're about ready to ride out," he told her, impressed by the change in her appearance.

"Do you think so? Really?" Francie's approval had been one thing, but she desperately needed her father's.

"Really," he assured her; then he teased, "You know, I always wanted a son, too."

"And I always did want to be a boy."

Charley knew that was true enough.

They both laughed.

"You do need one more thing—" He disappeared into his study for a moment and then came back carrying a gun and holster.

"If you're riding shotgun with me, you've got to be ready for trouble."

Dusty took the holster from him and set it aside on the table in the hall. "Papa—"

He heard the more serious note in her tone and looked her way, wondering if she was worried about leaving the following morning. "What, darling?"

"Can we go down to the cemetery one more time and tell Mama good-bye?"

"Let's go."

He put his arm around her and they left the house together.

In the predawn darkness the next morning, Dusty got dressed and strapped on the gun belt. As she grabbed up her gear and got ready to leave the house with her father, she knew her life was never going to be the same again.

Chapter Two

One Year Later

Texas Rangers Grant Spencer and Frank Thomas were after the deadly Les Jackson gang and believed they were closing in on the outlaws when they discovered the gang had split up. Grant's frustration was real as he studied the direction of their tracks.

"It looks like two of them headed toward Sunset, and the other two are riding north," Grant told Frank.

"They must know we're after them," Frank said.

"Good. I want them running scared." These outlaws were a bunch of thieves and murderers, and Grant wanted them brought to justice. "I'll go after the ones riding for Sunset."

"Be careful."

They both knew what a lawless, dangerous town Sunset was.

"Don't worry. I will. You watch out, too."

They shared a knowing look before riding their separate ways. They had long miles to cover, but they knew all the hardship would be worth it when they finally caught up with Jackson and his men and put an end to their killing ways.

It was much later that night when Les Jackson and Ugly Joe Williams sat around their small campfire unable to sleep.

"Who do you think is after us?" Ugly Joe worried.

"I'm thinking it's the Texas Rangers."

"The Rangers?" Ugly Joe grew nervous at the thought.

"Yeah. Whoever is on our trail don't quit easy and knows exactly what they're doing. This ain't no small-town posse," Les snarled in disgust. He'd always prided himself on being able to get clean away after one of his robberies or shoot-outs, and it infuriated him to be on the run after all these days.

"Maybe now that we've split up, we'll lose them," Ugly Joe hoped.

Les was quiet for a minute and then smiled coldly, suddenly wanting to get some revenge on the lawmen who were tracking them. "Or—maybe it's time for us to stop running."

Ugly Joe looked at him as if he were crazy. "What are you talking about? If these are Rangers—"

"Yeah, what if they are?"

"We got to keep moving. We got to outrun them. Besides, we have to meet up with Jim and Cale like we planned. They'll be expecting us, and if we don't show up on time, they might think something happened to us."

"Don't you worry. We'll be in Canyon Springs in plenty of time, but when we get to town, there won't be anybody on our trail."

Ugly Joe wasn't the brightest man around, but he finally figured out what Les was talking about. "So we're going to set a trap for them?"

"That's right," Les said, smiling real big. "And I know just the place where we can ambush whoever is tracking us—"

For the next day and a half, Frank stayed hard on the outlaws' trail. The loneliness of the hunt didn't bother him. He was used to being alone. He'd been on his own since he'd run away from home when he was twelve to escape his drunken, abusive father. His mother had run off the year before.

Frank concentrated on the job he had to do. It was important to stop the killers before anyone else was hurt. He was thankful that there had been no rain. The terrain was harsh and rugged, and a storm would have washed out the trail. He was cautious as he started up a narrow pathway along a steep drop-off, but even as alert as he was, Frank wasn't prepared for the ambush.

Les had set his trap perfectly.

He and Ugly Joe were waiting, hidden among the rocks up ahead, as the man who'd been trailing them came into view.

"I told you it was the Rangers tracking us," Les whispered to Ugly Joe as he made out the Ranger badge the lawman was wearing.

They both smiled evilly as they opened fire.

They saw the Ranger go for his gun, but they were too good. They watched in satisfaction as he was hit. His horse reared, throwing him off the side of the roadway. As the horse ran off, Les and Ugly Joe waited to make sure there were no other Rangers following behind. When they were certain that the man they'd shot had been tracking them alone, they hurried down to check on him.

"Nice shooting," Les told Ugly Joe as they looked over the edge. They could see the man, lying among the rocks about halfway down the rocky hillside.

"You want me to climb down there and make sure he ain't gonna give us any more trouble?"

"From the looks of him, he ain't going to be giving anybody any more trouble. Let's ride."

The two killers holstered their guns and went to where they'd left their horses. They mounted up and rode on. They were both feeling real good about the outcome of the ambush.

It was late, almost sundown, when Frank regained consciousness. He lay unmoving, staring around himself, completely at a loss. He couldn't remember anything—where he was or what he was doing there or even his own name—

The shock of his last realization jarred him deeply. He panicked and tried to sit up, only to groan in abject misery at his first attempt to move.

Pain radiated through him. His head was throbbing and his side ached. He'd had broken ribs before, and he recognized the agony of it. He lay still and shut his eyes again for a moment, trying to calm himself.

He opened his eyes and studied the jagged rocks and the steep hillside. He tried to be logical, but it wasn't easy. He felt a sudden need to take cover, to find a place out of sight and hide, but he didn't understand why. There was no one else around.

He was alone.

He saw no sign of his horse—if he'd even had a horse— Right then, he couldn't remember.

Frank lifted one hand to his forehead and found blood there. Ever so slowly, he levered himself onto one elbow and finally managed to sit up. Waves of dizziness left him even more disoriented as he managed to get to his feet. He stood there, lost and confused and weak. He knew there was no hope he could climb back up the hill, so he staggered down the slope, looking for anything that would help trigger his memory so he could piece together what had happened. He hadn't gone far when he lost his balance and fell again. He collapsed and lay still.

"Look!" young Andy Miller shouted to his sister when he caught sight of the man on the ground. "I told you I heard gunshots. There was trouble up here!"

Sarah saw the injured man who lay unmoving among the rocks.

"Come on," Sarah said, wheeling her horse around so they could find a way to reach him.

"What if he's an outlaw or something?" Andy worried.

"I guess we'll find out," she replied grimly as they rode into the rugged area.

Sarah dismounted and ran to kneel beside the man. She could see a lot of blood on his head and feared he was already dead. When she bent close, she was shocked to find he was still breathing.

"He's alive, Andy!"

Her brother hurried to help her.

Ever so carefully, she rolled the stranger onto his back, and it was then she saw his Ranger badge for the first time.

"He's a Ranger—" She looked up at her brother, shocked. "We have to get him back to the house—"

Her little brother was as surprised as she was to find out the stranger was a lawman. He looked nervously around. "Somebody must have ambushed him. What if they come back looking for him?"

She quickly unpinned the Ranger badge and put it in her pocket. "Come on, let's hurry and get him out of here while we can."

She knew the Ranger was lucky to be alive, but wounded and unconscious, he was helpless now. She realized he was a big man and it wasn't going to be easy to get him on one of their horses, but they had to move him—and fast. She checked him over to see whether he had any other bullet wounds, but found none. Relieved that there was still a chance they could save him, she took off his gun belt and carried it with her. They managed to lift him across the back of her horse and secured him there as best they could. The terrain was too rough to bring in their buckboard to transport him. Sarah rode double with Andy as they started slowly back toward the ranch house.

"Do you think he's going to die?" Andy asked worriedly.

"I hope not. We've got to do everything we can to save him."

"I wonder what Pa will say." He knew their father didn't take to having strangers around.

"We'll worry about that later."

Sarah was glad to find their father wasn't home when they reached the house. Chet, one of their ranch hands, saw them riding in and rushed out to help.

"Who is he? Is he dead?" Chet asked.

"No. We found him up in the ravine. Somebody ambushed him," she explained. "He's a Texas Ranger—"

"What?" The ranch hand was startled. He knew that could mean real trouble if the shooters came looking for the wounded stranger.

"I know." They shared an anxious look. "Let's get him inside."

Chet and Andy managed to carry the Ranger as Sarah went ahead of them to open the door. She put his gun belt and badge on the small table by the door and then led the way to her bedroom.

"My room will be easiest," Sarah said.

She quickly turned down the covers and stepped back as they lifted the Ranger onto the bed. Chet helped take his boots off.

"Thanks, Chet."

"Is there anything else you want me to do?"

"Just pray he makes it," she told him, "and keep an eye out for trouble."

"You think whoever shot him might still be around?"

"There's no telling—"

"Do you know where our pa is?" Andy asked as the ranch hand started to leave the house.

"He rode out earlier, but he didn't say where he was heading or when he'd be back."

Andy and Sarah knew when their father rode off that way, he was usually going into the nearby town of Eagle Ridge to drink and gamble. He'd been trying to lose himself in a bottle ever since their mother had left them some years before.

"Andy, stay with him while I put some water on to boil."

Sarah left the bedroom with Chet and went into the kitchen to get what she needed to tend to the injured man's wounds. She returned with a basin of water, washcloths and a towel, along with some salve and cloth to use as bandages. She realized then that the shirt he was wearing was covered with the dried blood.

"Andy, help me get his shirt off."

They carefully stripped off the shirt, revealing the broad, powerful width of his chest and shoulders. It was then she saw the bruising from his injured ribs. With utmost care, she set about cleaning his head wound. As she gently washed the blood from his face, she realized what a handsome man he was.

"He's real lucky to be alive, isn't he?" Andy said, knowing how close the Ranger had come to being killed.

"Yes, he is." She just hoped the handsome stranger was able to make a full recovery.

Sarah finished bandaging his head and then checked his ribs. With Andy's help, she tightly bound his chest to help them heal.

"What do we do now?" Andy asked.

She looked over at him. "There's nothing we can do but wait. Why don't you bring a chair in? That way one of us can sit with him in case he starts to stir. I wouldn't want him to wake up and try to get out of bed without help. He might fall again and hurt himself even worse."

Andy went out to get one of the chairs from the kitchen and put it next to the bed.

"I'll sit with him first," he offered.

"Thanks, Andy. I'll clean everything up and then see about starting dinner. Let's just hope Papa gets back before too late."

They knew the longer he stayed in town drinking, the meaner he would be when he showed up at the ranch. They'd never understood his drunken rages. They just knew it was safest to stay out of his way when he'd been drinking whiskey.

"Let me know if our Ranger starts to stir at all," she said.

"I will," Andy promised.

Chapter Three

Sunset, Texas

It was late when Texas Ranger Grant Spencer rode slowly down the dark, deserted main street of the lawless town. He spotted the Golden Nugget Saloon up ahead and reined in to dismount. He believed he was closing in on two of Les Jackson's gang of murdering thieves. The gunmen had a reputation for drinking and gambling, so Grant figured the saloon was the best place to start looking for them in the small town.

Determination filled Grant as he left his horse at the hitching rail and made his way up the street toward the saloon. If there was one thing he'd learned in his life, it was always to be ready for trouble, so he was cautious as he neared the entrance to the Golden Nugget.

The saloon was crowded and noisy inside. The piano player was playing a raucous tune while the scantily clad saloon girls strutted around the room, waiting on customers. Grant was glad it was busy for no one would notice him standing just outside the swinging doors, shielded by the cover of darkness. He wanted to take a look around the bar and see if he could spot any of the gunmen. They were all known to be quick on the draw, and Grant didn't want to give them any chance to go for their weapons.

Jim Harper, one of the fastest guns in Les Jackson's gang, was having a fine time in the saloon. Les had believed the law was closing in on them, so he'd had his men split up for a while with plans to meet again near Canyon Springs in a few weeks. Harper and Cale Pierce had initially ridden off together, but they had parted ways not too long before.

Harper had wanted to come to town and enjoy himself for a while, and Cale had wanted to keep riding. Harper was confident they'd outrun whoever had been tracking them, and so he had come into Sunset that afternoon ready to do some serious celebrating at the Golden Nugget. The town was known for its lawless ways, so he believed he could relax and enjoy himself there for a few days. He had been drinking heavily ever since. When the buxom blonde saloon girl he'd heard called "Sugar" sashayed past his table, he caught her by the arm and pulled her down onto his lap, enjoying the feel of her lush curves pressed tight against him. He thought Cale had been a fool for moving on. The man didn't know what he was missing. He was going to have one fine time with the curvy blonde.

"You looking to have some fun tonight, Sugar?" he asked, his gaze going over her hungrily.

"You know I am," she purred and leaned closer

so he could get a better view of her cleavage, amply displayed by the low-cut neckline of her red satin gown. She'd been watching this man ever since he'd come into the saloon. He wasn't the cleanest man there, but he obviously had money, and money could make her forgive a lot of faults—even smelly ones. "Don't you think I look like fun?"

"Oh, yeah," he drooled, ready to take her straight upstairs. "You look like a lot of fun—"

"But can you afford me?" she taunted, drawing back a little to tease him and entice him. "I don't come cheap—or easy."

"Oh, yeah, I got the money." Harper pulled a wad of cash from his pocket and stuffed it down the bodice of her dress. "And I always did like a challenge—"

"Well, big guy," Sugar chuckled sensuously as she kissed him hotly on the mouth, "you just bought yourself one. I sure hope you're up to it."

"Oh, I am."

"How long you gonna be in town?"

"Long enough to take care of you—I don't have to be in Canyon Springs for better than a week."

"I may just keep you upstairs that long," she purred, liking the depth of his pockets.

She stood and drew him up with her.

Harper didn't need any encouraging. He was more than ready to make her earn her pay.

Sugar led the way toward the staircase to the second floor with Harper following close behind. When they reached the bottom of the steps, he didn't waste any time. He swept her up into his arms, ready to carry her upstairs. He had just started to kiss her again when he heard a voice call out from behind him.

"Don't move, Harper."

Grant had spotted the outlaw right away. He'd seen no sign of any other gunman in the saloon, so he'd decided to take on Harper while he was being distracted by the saloon girl.

At the sound of the command, Harper stopped right where he was. His mood suddenly sobered as he realized he was in trouble—big trouble. He'd thought he'd gotten clean away, but he knew now he'd been a fool to let his guard down tonight. He immediately regretted all the heavy drinking he'd been doing, and he immediately regretted not staying with Cale. But regrets didn't do him any good now.

Chaos reigned in the Golden Nugget as everyone scrambled to get out of the way. Chairs and tables were overturned in the rush.

Ken, the bartender, didn't recognize the man who'd come into the saloon with his revolver drawn, and he started to reach down for the shotgun he kept hidden behind the bar for moments just like this.

"He's a Ranger," one of the customers yelled to Ken, after spotting the badge the stranger was wearing.

Ken forgot about getting his shotgun and stepped back to let the Ranger take charge and do his job.

Desperation and panic filled Harper at the realization that it was a Ranger who had tracked him down.

Grant slowly crossed the room, closing in on him. "Put the girl down and turn around. Don't make any fast moves," he ordered.

At his command, Sugar all but tore herself loose from Harper's arms and threw herself out of harm's way.

Freed from the distraction of the dance hall girl's lush nearness, the outlaw turned to face the Ranger.

"There must be some mistake," Harper said calmly, stalling for time as he tried to figure out what to do.

"I don't make mistakes, Harper." Grant kept his gun aimed straight at the killer. "Toss your gun aside."

Harper acted as if he was going to do what the Ranger had ordered, but, in truth, he wasn't about to go down that easy. He knew his best chance of making a run for it was right there in the crowded saloon. Unwilling to give himself up without a fight, he went for his gun as he dove to the side, hoping to find some cover among the tables before the Ranger could react.

But Grant was ready.

The instant the gunman made his move to escape, Grant got off a shot.

His aim proved true.

Harper collapsed on the saloon floor.

Grant moved to stand over the dead outlaw, satisfied that Jim Harper wouldn't be killing any more innocent people.

"He should have listened when I gave an order," Grant said coldly as he picked up the outlaw's discarded gun and shoved it in his waistband.

"Who was he?" Ken asked as he came to stand at Grant's side.

"Jim Harper."

Ken instantly recognized his name. "He was one of the Jackson gang, wasn't he?"

"That's right. How long has he been in town?"

"He just rode in today."

"Was anyone else with him?"

"No, he rode in alone," Sugar offered as she came over to join them. "So he was part of that gang?"

"That's right. Did he mention that he might be meeting up with anyone?" Grant asked.

"He was all about drinking tonight," she told the lawman, and then remembered something Harper had said. "He did mention that he didn't have to be in Canyon Springs for another week."

Canyon Springs—

Grant nodded and looked at the bartender. "You got an undertaker in town?"

"We sure do."

Ken sent one of his customers after the undertaker, and the fellow quickly showed up to haul the gunman's body away.

Grant went along with the undertaker. He wanted to go through the outlaw's belongings to see if he could find any other clues to where the rest of the gang might be hiding out.

Sugar stood off to the side of the room with her friend Annie, watching as they took the dead man out of the saloon. She had worked in the Golden Nugget for quite a while and had seen a lot of wild things, but she had been shocked by what had just happened.

"I had no idea he was a killer—" she told her friend.

"Thank heaven the Ranger showed up when he did," Annie said.

"You're right about that." She shuddered at the thought of being upstairs alone with a vicious killer. "I sure would like to buy that handsome Ranger a drink if he comes back in." The thought of spending time with the good-looking lawman eased her tense mood.

"Not if I get to him first," Annie challenged with a sly grin.

"Let's just hope we get the chance."

They were both smiling at the thought as they went back to work.

After leaving the undertaker, Grant took his horse down to the livery to stable it for the night and then went to the hotel to take a room. First thing in the morning, he would send a wire to his captain to let him know Jim Harper wouldn't be causing any more trouble and that he would be headed for Canyon Springs on the trail of the rest of the gang. He hoped the information he'd gotten from the saloon girl was reliable, for he'd found no clues to the gang's whereabouts among the outlaw's possessions.

As he bedded down for the night, Grant found himself wondering how Frank was doing tracking the other members of the gang.

Chapter Four

It was getting late when Sarah sent Andy on to bed and took up her vigil at the wounded Ranger's bedside. Their father hadn't returned from Eagle Ridge yet, and she knew there would be trouble when he finally did come home, but for the moment, the only thing that really mattered was keeping watch over the injured man. She would worry about her father later.

Ever so gently, Sarah touched the Ranger's forehead. She was relieved to find he hadn't developed a fever. She turned the lamp on the bedside table down to a softer glow and sat back in the chair to keep watch over him.

Frank regained consciousness slowly, coming back from the peace of oblivion to the agony of reality. The throbbing in his head was nearly unbearable.

A sudden sense of panic filled him—

There was danger—

Something was wrong—

He opened his eyes and looked around to find himself in a darkened room that he had never seen before. His panic worsened, and he was suddenly sure he needed to get out of there fast!

He tried to move, but the pain in his side stopped him cold, and a low groan of pure misery escaped him as he fell back on the bed.

Sarah had dozed off for a moment. The sound of the Ranger's groan startled her—and thrilled her—for she knew it meant he was finally coming around.

"You're awake— Thank God—"

The sound of the unknown feminine voice so close beside him shocked Frank, and he looked over to find a beautiful, fair-haired young woman sitting by the bedside. He frowned.

"Who are you?" he asked, confused. She was so pretty, he knew he certainly would have remembered her if he'd ever seen her before. He tried to lever himself up on his elbow, but she put a hand on his shoulder to stop him from moving.

"Stay still. You've been hurt. My name's Sarah."

He looked up at her as he lay back, trying to place her, but he had no memory of ever meeting her before. Yet here he was lying in a bed with her sitting beside him. "Should I know you?"

"No— I'll tell you everything that happened, but, first, tell me—what's your name?"

For one long moment, his dark-eyed gaze met hers, and she could see the haunted look in his eyes.

Frank desperately searched for a clue to his own identity, but his mind was a total blank. "I don't know," he answered honestly.

"What?" Sarah was stunned by his revelation.

Frank lifted one hand to his head and realized he was bandaged. "I have no memory of anything— What happened to me?"

"My brother Andy and I heard some gunshots, and we went to see what was going on. We found you at the bottom of a ravine. Someone had shot you and then your horse must have thrown you. Luckily, the bullet had just grazed your head."

Believing someone was out to kill him, he knew he had to take action. "I've got to get away from here— They might be still out there—"

"No, don't try to get up— Please—" She pressed him back down again. "You've been here for hours now, and no one has shown up. We didn't see anybody near where we found you either. Whoever shot you must have gone on, thinking you were dead."

Frank was surprised by how weak he was. The pain in his side was excruciating, not to mention his headache.

"Here—let me show you something. It might help you remember—" Sarah went out into the front hall and got his Ranger badge from where she'd left it on the table. She came back into the bedroom and handed it to him. "You're a Ranger. You were wearing this when we found you to-day."

Frank frowned as he stared at the Texas Ranger badge. He concentrated, trying to remember anything that would help him recall his past, but there was nothing except the pain that ravaged him. "I don't remember—" He gripped the badge in his hand, a tortured look on his face.

Sarah understood his misery and wanted to help, but she knew there was little she could do at that moment. "The best thing for you to do right now is rest," she told him. "Your memory will return. It's just a matter of time."

"I hope you're right—"

"Do you want something to eat or drink?"

"Water—"

She quickly brought him a glass of water and helped him sit up slightly so he could take a few sips. Just that little exertion exhausted him and he lay back wearily on the bed.

"I'll be right here if you need anything," she said, starting to move away.

Frank looked over at her again. "Sarah—"

She quickly turned back to him, thinking something was wrong.

"Thank you."

Sarah gently touched his arm. "I'm just glad we found you in time."

"So am I."

They said no more as he closed his eyes, seeking release from the pain.

It was almost midnight when Sarah heard her father ride up to the house. She slipped quickly from her bedroom, closing the door quietly behind her so the Ranger wouldn't be disturbed.

"What's going on? What the hell are you doing up this late?" Nat Miller snarled as he staggered into the house to find his daughter still up and fully dressed.

"Waiting to talk to you, Papa. Something happened while you were gone, and I wanted to tell you about it right away."

Nat swore vilely as he threw his hat aside. It was then he noticed the strange gun belt on the hall table.

"What's this doing here?"

"It belongs to the Ranger—"

"Ranger?" He frowned.

"Papa, let's go into the kitchen. We have to talk."

Nat realized that she'd closed her bedroom door when she'd come out, and he stomped over to open it. The sight that greeted him was a shock. There was a half-dressed strange man lying unconscious in his daughter's bed. He could see the bandages on the man's head and chest and he wondered what in the world had happened while he'd been gone.

"Get into the kitchen," he ordered, shutting the door again.

He followed Sarah there and sat down facing her at the table.

"I want to know everything—now!" The last thing he'd wanted tonight was trouble. He'd done his drinking and he'd even won a little playing poker. He'd been feeling half good until he'd come home to this—

"I was out riding with Andy and we heard some gunshots. We went to check and found the Ranger unconscious in a ravine. He was lucky to be alive. Whoever ambushed him just barely missed killing him. The bullet grazed his head, and then his horse must have thrown him."

"How do you know he's a Ranger?" Nat challenged.

"He was wearing his badge," she told him.

"So, has he come to yet?"

"Yes. He woke up for a little while earlier."

"What did he say?"

"Not much. I think he has amnesia," Sarah said. "He couldn't even remember his own name. I gave him his badge, thinking it might jar his memory, but it didn't help. He couldn't remember anything. It was a little frightening for him."

Nat wasn't happy about the state of things, but, even drunk as he was, he knew there was nothing more he could do that night.

"You go wake your brother up. I don't want you in a bedroom at night with a strange man. I don't care if he's injured or not. It ain't right."

She started to tell him Andy hadn't been in bed all that long, but knew what would happen if she tried to contradict one of her father's orders when he was drunk. "Yes, Papa."

"I'm going to bed. You make sure I ain't woke up in the morning."

"Yes, Papa." She watched him disappear into his own room and shut the door. Then she hurried off to wake Andy.

Her brother was sleepy, but he understood why she was getting him up. Neither one of them ever wanted to rile their father when he'd been drinking. She told him all that had happened.

"What do I do if the Ranger wakes up again?"

"Come and get me right away. I'll be in your room."

Andy went to keep watch over the wounded man, while Sarah sought what rest she could in her brother's bedroom. But even as tired as she was, sleep would not come. Her concern for the Ranger troubled her. She worried that if the ones who'd tried to kill him learned he was still alive, they would come back looking for him to finish the job. Somehow, she had to convince her father to let him stay on the ranch until his memory returned. Only that way could the man be safe.

It was daylight when Frank awoke to find himself alone in the strange bedroom. He lay there for a long moment, trying to remember how he'd come to be there—what had happened—but there was nothing. His only memory was of the girl named Sarah who'd been by his side the night before and who had told him he was a Texas Ranger. He lifted the badge that he still held clutched in his hand to look at it, but it stirred nothing within him.

His whole life was a blank.

It was as if he'd never existed before now.

A moment of panic threatened Frank. His head was still pounding and his side hurt. He knew only that he'd been injured, nothing else.

Determination filled him. He couldn't just lie there. He had to move. It took all the strength he could draw upon, but he did it. He managed to swing his long legs over the side of the bed and sit up. A wave of dizziness swept over him, and he rested his head in his hands as he fought for control.

"You're moving—" Sarah had been cooking breakfast for Andy and had decided to look in on him. She was glad she had as she hurried to his side. He looked as if he was still in a lot of pain. "Are you all right?"

Frank lifted his head to find the girl he remembered coming toward him. He was glad to see her again. Her pretty face gave him something to focus on.

"I think so," he managed.

She reached out and put her hand to his cheek.

For a moment, he was surprised by her gentle touch, but her next words explained everything.

"You don't have a fever and that's good, but even so, it's going to take you a while to recover, so don't try to do too much right away. You're still weak."

"I just found that out," he agreed.

"I'm cooking breakfast. Are you up to eating something?"

"Yes, please."

"Good." Sarah knew it was a positive sign that he was hungry. "Sit back on the bed. I'll bring it in to you."

He did as he'd been ordered, and as the delicious aroma from the kitchen made its way through the house, he knew he was in for a treat.

"Here you are," Sarah said, returning to the bedroom several minutes later carrying a plate piled high with food. A young man followed behind her with a cup of coffee for him. She handed him the plate.

"This is my brother Andy," she explained, nodding at the young man.

"Glad to meet you." After shaking Andy's hand, Frank stared down at the home-cooked food. It had been a long time since he'd enjoyed a meal like this one. There were fried eggs, bacon, fried potatoes and biscuits.

As Andy put the coffee on the small bedside table, he saw the look on the Ranger's face and hurried to reassure him, "My sis is a good cook."

"I wasn't worried about that," Frank said, managing a half smile. "I was just wondering if there was more where this came from."

"Ranger, if you want more, just say the word," Sarah told him. "It's good that you've got an appetite."

"With cooking like this, who wouldn't?" He started to eat, then turned to Andy. "You were with your sister when she rescued me, right?"

"Yes, sir."

"Well, thank you for all your help."

Andy smiled at him. "I'm just glad you're better."

"So am I."

Andy and Sarah went back to the kitchen to eat their own breakfasts.

"What are we going to do about him?" Andy asked, looking up at his sister with all the concern he felt showing in his eyes.

"Until he's stronger, he needs to stay here with us so he'll be safe."

"I know," Andy agreed. "I'm worried about him, not knowing who he is and all. That's got to be hard for him."

"I know. We'll talk to Papa about it when he gets up."

They both knew it would be hard convincing their father to help the man. Their father wasn't known for his kindness or generosity with strangers, but still, since this man was a Texas Ranger, they hoped that would make a difference.

Andy had just come back in the kitchen after getting the Ranger's dishes when their father appeared in the doorway. They were surprised that he was up so early. Usually after a night in town, he slept well into the afternoon, but not today.

"Is he awake?" Nat demanded of them.

"Yes, Papa," Andy answered quickly. "And he managed to eat his breakfast, too."

"Then I think I need to have a talk with him." Nat turned and headed toward the bedroom.

Sarah and Andy quickly followed.

"Young man, I think we need to talk," Nat said gruffly as he walked right into the bedroom without announcing himself. He found the stranger sitting up in bed. Nat took note of his bandaged chest and head, and he knew Sarah hadn't been exaggerating when she'd told him how close the Ranger had come to being killed.

Frank tensed as he looked over at the man, but said nothing for the time being.

"I'm Nat Miller. This here is my ranch—the Circle M."

Frank nodded slightly. "I appreciate your family helping me this way. There's no telling what might have happened to me if Sarah and Andy hadn't brought me back here."

Nat stood looking down at him. "My daughter says you're a Ranger."

"That's what she told me, but I have no memory of anything before yesterday when I woke up here," Frank answered honestly.

"Nothing at all? Not your name? Or who might have been trying to kill you? I don't need no trouble here on the ranch." Nat studied the wounded man, watching to see if he was lying.

Frank looked up at him and met his gaze straight on. "No. Nothing."

Nat appreciated that the man looked him in the eye. He knew then he wasn't a liar. "All right. You're welcome to stay here for as long as you need to, and we won't go telling anybody that you're here, just in case someone is out gunning for you. The fewer people who know where you are, the better."

"I appreciate it."

"You rest up." Nat turned and left the room.

Frank watched him go, and then closed his eyes in frustration as he tried desperately to remember something that would give him a clue to his identity.

Chapter Five

One Week Later

"Oh, Dusty, you look so pretty in that dress!" Francie told her friend as she watched Dusty standing before the mirror in her bedroom wearing the borrowed turquoise gown.

"I feel pretty, too—for the first time in ages—" Dusty admitted. "Are you sure it's all right if I wear your gown tonight?"

"Of course, it is! I'm just thrilled it fits you so well," Francie insisted, delighted that Dusty was in town and would be able to attend the dance. It wasn't often Dusty and her father managed to get back in time for the social events of Canyon Springs. True, they had to head out again the following day, but at least her friend could have fun tonight.

Dusty had been wearing her pants and work shirt, as usual, when she'd first come to the house for a visit, and Francie, good friend that she was, had insisted Dusty come to her room and pick out one of her dresses to wear.

Dusty stared at her own reflection in the mirror

once more and then looked at her friend and grinned. "You know, I actually feel like a girl again— even with the short hair—" She twirled about, enjoying the feel of the skirt flaring out around her. She rarely bothered to wear a dress anymore. The only time she did was when she and her father happened to be in town on a Sunday and she got to go to church. The simple dress she wore then was nothing like the gown she had on now. The lovely turquoise confection had a scooped neckline and yards of lace trim.

"You are a girl, and don't you ever forget it!" her friend scolded, and they both laughed.

"It's been so long since I've had the chance to dress up—" Dusty turned to get an even better view of the stylish gown.

"Well, this is your big night. We're going to have a good time."

"I know."

"I just wish you were in town more."

"I do, too, but my father wants me to stay with him."

Francie understood, but knew it was a difficult life for her friend. "I'm just thankful that you haven't had any trouble on your trips."

"Oh, we've run into trouble, but Papa's one of the best drivers around. He can handle just about anything. Why, just last week one of the wheels was damaged, and we almost tipped over."

Francie gasped at the thought of Dusty sitting on the driver's bench when the stage started to go over. "What did you do?"

"I held on real tight," Dusty answered, managing a grin even as she remembered the terror of the moment, "and Papa straightened it out. No one was hurt. Some of the passengers were a little shaken up, but they got over it."

"You are so brave. I don't know how you do it."

"I'm my father's daughter."

"Your mother would be proud of you."

For a moment, Dusty was quiet. "I hope so."

"She would be," Francie reassured her and gave her a quick hug.

Dusty started to tell her that the stage would be carrying a big payroll when they left in the morning and that her father had even hired an extra man to ride along with them, but she decided against it. The fewer people who knew about the money they were transporting, the better.

"Well, let's forget all about you riding shotgun and think about you dancing tonight."

"Riding shotgun might be easier."

Francie laughed, then paused to study Dusty thoughtfully. "Now, we need to find you a necklace to wear with that gown."

"Jewelry?"

"Of course! We need just the right finishing touch to your outfit."

"I guess so," Dusty agreed. Then she asked a bit self-consciously as she glanced back at her mirror image and grimaced a bit at the sight of her short-cropped tresses, "Do you think any of the ladies will say something about my hair?" She knew how disapproving the town's matrons could be.

"Not if we fix it up real pretty—"

"But how? It's so short—"

"I've got an idea. Sit down for a minute," Francie directed, pointing to the chair in front of her small vanity.

Dusty did as she was told and waited while her friend went to open one of her dresser drawers.

"This should do it," Francie said with confidence as she took out a length of white ribbon along with some hairpins. She grabbed her brush and comb and went to work. A few minutes later, she stepped back to critically study her creation. She'd tied a fashionable bow out of the ribbon and had artfully pinned it in the back of Dusty's hair, so it appeared she had longer hair that she was wearing styled up. "What do you think?"

"I don't believe it—" Dusty stared at her own reflection and smiled. "It won't come loose on me, will it?"

"I pinned it up as best I could. As long as you don't do anything too wild tonight, it should stay in."

Dusty impulsively got up and gave her friend a big hug. "You're right. We are going to have a good time! And the ladies are going to think I look most proper, thanks to you."

"They're going to be glad to see you. They often ask me about you and want to make sure you're all right."

Relief swept through Dusty, and she was smiling again. It had been so long since she'd enjoyed any of the social activities in town.

Francie went on, "Now, let's get you a necklace and a pair of shoes—"

Dusty laughed out loud as she lifted up her skirt to reveal her work boots. "You don't like me wearing these with the gown?"

"Nobody would see them, but I don't think you'd be too comfortable trying to dance in them."

"I could do it," she teased.

"I'm sure you could, but just for tonight, I want you to wear a pair of my shoes and be a lady from head to toe—"

"Oh, all right," Dusty agreed.

They were laughing again as they set about picking out a pair of shoes for her. They could hardly wait for the evening to come.

A short time later as they both put the finishing touches on their appearances, Dusty went to stand in front of the mirror.

"Do you think my father will recognize me when he shows up?" She had grown so accustomed to thinking of herself as her father's "kid," the girl staring back at her in the mirror amazed her.

Papa had told her he would meet her at the Randolph house and they would all go over to the social together.

"I think we'll find out real soon. He should be showing up anytime now," Francie said. "This look is definitely a change for you, that's for sure." She admired the way the gown fit her friend and the sparkle of the necklace they'd picked out that set off the demure neckline of the dress. "You're probably going to have all the boys chasing you tonight."

"Even the new banker?" Dusty teased. Francie had mentioned that she thought him most handsome, so she knew her friend was interested in the young man.

"He'd better not!" Francie exclaimed, giving her friend a daring look. "I'd hate to have to fight you over him."

"Dressed like this, I'm not sure I could take you on," Dusty laughed. "What did you say his name was?"

"His name is Rick Washburn and he is so handsome."

"Have you gotten to know him very well?"

"We've only had the chance to talk a few times, but tonight may just be the night."

Francie's mother appeared in the doorway then. "Ladies, it's time to leave. Your fathers are waiting for you in the parlor." She smiled warmly at Dusty. "You both look absolutely beautiful, and, Dusty, I love how you fixed your hair."

Coming from Mrs. Randolph, the compliment was high praise. "Thank you, but I didn't do it. Francie did."

"Well, it looks very pretty." Marlene Randolph gave them each a quick kiss on the cheek and ushered them from the room to meet their fathers. "Now, remember. You're to behave like perfect ladies tonight."

Both girls agreed demurely as she led them into the parlor.

"Well, gentlemen, we're ready to go," Mrs. Randolph announced.

Charley and Fred Randolph had been deep in conversation, and they looked up as the women came into the room.

The sight of Dusty all dressed up, and looking so much like her mother, stunned Charley. He hurt deep inside as he realized how much he still missed his wife. He knew he always would. Somehow, he managed to keep his pain hidden from his daughter as he gave her an approving smile. "You look lovely."

"Do you really think so?" Dusty asked, smoothing her skirt a bit self-consciously.

"Absolutely," he assured her.

"We've got us some fine-looking women," Fred remarked, going to kiss his wife.

"Yes, we do."

"I think we're going to have our hands full making sure the boys behave themselves around our girls tonight," Fred said as he escorted his wife and daughter from the house.

Charley and Dusty followed them as they headed for the town hall where the dance was being held.

The hall was crowded and the musicians were just starting up a new tune as they went in.

"I'm claiming you for your first dance, otherwise I may not get the chance," Charley told Dusty as he guided her directly out onto the dance floor.

She was laughing as he squired her about.

Francie stood with her parents at the side of the room, watching them.

"Well, who wants to dance with me first?" Fred asked, looking between his two lovely ladies.

"I do, Papa," Francie quickly answered. "I can't let Dusty have all the fun."

They joined the others on the dance floor, leaving Marlene smiling in delight at their father/daughter dance.

When the tune ended, the girls started off to visit with some of their friends, while Fred claimed his wife for the next dance.

Dusty and Francie hadn't gone far when two hands from a local ranch, Jack Bryan and Steve Wilson, caught up with them.

"Would you ladies like to dance?" they invited.

"We'd love to!" Francie answered for them both.

Never known for her shyness, she took Jack's arm without hesitation and went with him to join the other couples on the dance floor while Steve claimed Dusty.

"Well, look who's all dressed up tonight," Madeline Jones, the blonde and beautiful daughter of the local doctor, said cattily to Caroline O'Hara, one of the other girls from town.

"How did you even recognize her?" Caroline giggled, being equally hateful about Dusty's appearance. She was Madeline's closest friend and always agreed with everything she said.

"I know. Why, she almost looks like a girl tonight—instead of a boy. I wonder how long it took her to fix herself up this way?"

"It must have taken hours—or maybe days—"

They shared a sneering look as they watched

Dusty dancing. They were both jealous that Jack and Steve had chosen to dance with other girls.

Charley stood at the side of the room for a while, watching Dusty. He kept his expression carefully guarded, but deep within, his pain grew. He'd hardly attended any social functions since his wife's death, and he found himself regretting now that he'd come tonight. Unable to bear his loneliness any longer, he sought Fred out and told him that he would be back in a little while. Then he left the hall. He knew that as long as the Randolphs were there, Dusty would be safe.

He headed straight for the saloon.

He had some heavy drinking to do.

"There he is—" Francie whispered to Dusty a short time later, her heartbeat quickening as she caught sight of Rick Washburn.

"That's your banker?" Dusty asked eagerly as she studied the darkly handsome, well-dressed man.

"Yes," her friend replied dreamily as she watched him across the room.

"He is good-looking," Dusty agreed.

"And he's going to be mine, so don't go getting any ideas," Francie declared, staking out her territory.

Dusty only laughed at her friend. "You don't have to worry about me."

"Well, you do look awfully pretty tonight—"

"Thanks to you."

They shared a laugh together just as their favorite dance—the "ladies' choice"—was announced.

Dusty looked at her friend encouragingly. "Hurry! Go get your Rick before one of the other girls does!"

"'My Rick'—" Francie repeated. "I like the sound of that." She didn't need any more encouragement. She hurried off to claim him for the dance.

Dusty watched as Francie approached the banker. She was delighted to see that he smiled down at her friend and quickly took her up on her offer. She knew Francie was in heaven as she watched her move about the dance floor in his arms. He seemed quite taken with her, and Dusty couldn't wait to talk to her friend later and hear all the details.

Dusty thought about asking someone to dance, but just then she caught sight of the elderly town matrons seated across the room, watching the couples on the dance floor. Her mother had been good friends with the white-haired, portly Miss Gertrude Stevens so she sought her out for a visit.

"Dusty, darling, it is so good to see you," Miss Gertrude told her, reaching out to take her hand and draw Dusty down to sit on the seat beside her.

"It's good to see you, too, Miss Gertrude," Dusty responded with heartfelt enthusiasm.

"You look very pretty this evening," the older woman complimented her.

Dusty actually blushed a bit, knowing it was high praise coming from Miss Gertrude. "Thank you. Francie helped me get ready. She did a fine job on my hair, don't you think?"

"Yes, she did," Miss Gertrude said approvingly.

"We were all just saying how glad we are that you finally managed to be in town for a dance so we could visit with you. Isn't that right, Betty?" Miss Gertrude turned to a friend who was sitting on the opposite side of her.

"That's right."

"So why didn't you claim one of these handsome young men for the dance?" Miss Gertrude asked.

Dusty smiled. "Because I wanted to visit with you."

"Well, I'm glad you did."

"We've been missing you and wondering how you've been doing," Betty put in. "How are you?"

"Papa and I are doing fine."

"It's a shame your father can't find some other way to make a living," Betty criticized. She was known as a woman who always said what she thought. "It just doesn't seem civilized for you to be out riding around all the time, dressed like a boy."

Dusty couldn't help smiling. Betty didn't know the half of what went on during the stagecoach runs, and she wasn't about to tell her. "There are difficult times, but we manage. And, honestly, I can't imagine my father doing anything else."

"I know," Miss Gertrude sympathized. "Your mother used to say the same thing about him. He's a man who loves adventure."

"Yes, he is," Dusty agreed, and she realized then that she truly was her father's daughter. As much as she'd enjoyed dressing up that evening and attending the dance, she honestly felt more like herself when she was working with her father on the stage. She glanced around, realizing then that she hadn't seen him for a while, and she wondered where he'd gone. She was about to excuse herself and go look for him when the ladies' choice dance ended, and Ted Anderson sought her out.

"Come on, Dusty," the ranch hand said. "It's time I got a dance with you tonight! See you later, ladies," he told the elderly women as he whisked Dusty away.

"You'd *better* see me later, Ted," Miss Gertrude teasingly called after him. "I'm expecting to dance with you myself!"

"I'll be back for you real soon, Miss Gertrude!" he promised.

"I'm counting on it, young man!"

Betty couldn't help laughing at her outrageous friend. There was never a dull moment when Miss Gertrude was around, that was for sure, and that was why she loved her so much.

Chapter Six

"You're doing some serious drinking tonight, ain't you?" remarked Sam, the bartender at the Trail's End, as he poured Charley yet another straight shot of his best whiskey. Rowdy cowboys had been coming in all night, and Sam was used to their behavior, but he knew it was unusual for Charley to drink so heavily.

"Sometimes a man just needs some good whiskey," Charley said, downing the liquor and shoving the glass back across the bar for another refill.

"What's on your mind?" Sam knew Charley had to be troubled about something, for he'd been drinking steadily ever since he'd come in almost an hour before.

"Nothing." His answer was terse.

Sam knew then there was no point in trying to get more out of him. "Aren't you heading out again soon?"

"In the morning—early," Charley muttered. Then forgetting his determination to keep the news of the payroll he was carrying quiet, he offered, "I've got a big payroll to transport on this run, so we're taking an extra guard with us."

"Good. You be careful."

"We will be."

Sam went to wait on some wild cowboys who'd just come in while Charley continued drinking. This was the first time Sam had heard of Charley carrying a payroll. He found the news interesting.

There was a stranger who'd been drinking quietly at the far end of the bar. He'd heard Charley's mention of the payroll and thought the news was interesting, too. Without drawing any attention to himself, he finished off his drink and left the bar, disappearing into the night.

Grant could hear the sounds of music and revelry as he rode slowly down the main street of Canyon Springs, and he realized something was going on that night. He knew he'd have to check it out eventually, but first he wanted to stop at the saloon. He believed Jackson and his gang would be more likely to be drinking than dancing—if they'd made it to town already.

Grant had taken off his Ranger badge before he'd reached town. For now, he wanted to blend in and go unnoticed. Les Jackson, Ugly Joe Williams and Cale Pierce were in the area or would be real soon, and he was going to be ready and waiting for them.

Reining in near the Trail's End, Grant tied up his horse and stood there for a moment just looking around. Other than the big dance that was going on, the streets seemed quiet enough, so he moved on toward the saloon. He glanced in the window before entering, wanting to make sure he wasn't in for any surprises, but he saw no sign of the gang. Glad to have a chance to relax for at least a little while, he went in, more than ready for a drink.

"What'll it be?" Sam asked as he moved to wait on the tall, lean stranger who'd just come to stand at the bar.

"Whiskey," Grant told him, taking note of his surroundings. There were several men drinking at the bar, a few gaudily dressed saloon girls working the tables, and some gamblers playing poker in the back of the room. It looked like a typical Friday night in any saloon, though not quite as crowded as it could be.

Sam quickly set a glass before him and filled it with the potent liquor. "You just ride in?"

"Yeah." Grant paid the bartender and took a deep drink. "Looks like you've got some excitement going on tonight."

"It's the dance down at the hall. The boys look forward to this one all year. Business is a little slow now, but it'll pick up later."

"I'll have to head over and have some fun myself."

"You'll find lots of pretty girls," Sam assured him, wondering what business the new man had there in Canyon Springs. "You just passing through or are you planning to stay a while?"

"I haven't really decided yet. Is there a hotel in town?"

"Just two blocks down," Sam answered as he went to wait on other customers.

Grant took his time finishing his drink. After the long ride in, he would have enjoyed just staying there and drinking for the rest of the night, but it was too soon to let his guard down completely. He had to take a look around at the dance and make sure he really had beaten Jackson and his men to town.

Grant left the saloon a few minutes later. After taking care of his horse, he got his gear and went down to the hotel to find a place to stay. As he let himself into his room, he was glad to see the hotel was a clean one. The thought of finally sleeping in a real bed later that night definitely appealed to him after all the nights on the trail. Knowing it was getting late and he didn't have a lot of time, he quickly washed his face and hands and changed shirts before heading over to the dance.

Francie and Dusty were both trying to catch their breath after a particularly rousing dance when Mark Wagner and Paul Stanford, two hands from a nearby ranch, approached them.

"C'mon, Francie," Paul said, taking her by the arm. "This dance is mine!"

Paul was good-looking enough, but Francie could smell the liquor on him and wanted to decline.

"Well, I was—"

"Come on, little honey. We're going to have us a good time."

She had no chance to avoid him as he pulled her out onto the dance floor.

Dusty had sensed her friend's hesitation, but before she could do anything, Mark grabbed her. Dusty knew Mark was a real bad dancer, so she had to pay attention and concentrate on avoiding injury as he took her in his arms.

Paul had had his eye on Francie for some time now. He knew her family had money, so he was thinking she'd be a good catch for a poor cowboy. He planned to maneuver her outside away from the hall and set about seriously trying to woo her tonight. He had to admit he had been surprised by how pretty Dusty looked tonight. He hadn't seen her wearing a dress in quite a while, but that didn't matter to him. He was after money, and that came with Francie.

The tune was a rousing one, and Paul grinned. The lively dancing would make it easier to get Francie over to the far side of the room, away from her parents.

Francie knew Paul was dancing a little wildly, but she attributed that to the liquor he'd been drinking. She managed to keep up with him and keep a smile on her face at the same time. As awkward as she was feeling with Paul, she knew Dusty had it much worse with Mark. She'd already danced with Mark once tonight and had a sore toe to prove it.

"C'mon," Paul said in a low voice, and in one

quick move he managed to whirl her right out the back door.

"Paul—what are you doing?"

"I thought a little cool night air might feel good right now. What about you?" he asked, keeping hold of her hand as he drew her away from the light of the hall and into the surrounding darkness.

"I really need to get back inside. My parents will be wondering where I've gone. They'll worry about me."

"There's nothing to worry about, darling," he said, stopping and smiling down at her now that they were out of sight. "You're with me."

"This is most—"

She never got to finish her sentence. Paul pulled her close and kissed her, his mouth covering hers in a hungry, sloppy, devouring kiss.

Francie had long fantasized about a romantic embrace in the dark shadows of the night. She'd imagined being swept off her feet by her hero, who would declare his love and propose. Never in all her fairy-tale daydreams had she dreamed that the man kissing her would smell like whiskey or be so rough with her.

Paul felt her resistance, but that only made him tighten his grip on her. He was confident his romantic ways would win her over.

"Let me go—" she gasped when she finally managed to break off the kiss.

"You know you're lovin' it," he told her, pulling her tightly against him again.

"No, I'm not!" Francie hissed, trying to twist away from him. "Stop it!"

"Aw, honey—"

"Don't—"

"You heard what Francie said. Let her go," Rick directed. He'd been on his way over to ask Francie for another dance, but the ranch hand had gotten to her first. He had been disappointed, but had planned to claim her for the next one, until he'd seen Paul all but drag her out the back door. He'd known then something was wrong.

Paul was angered by the interruption. He kept a tight hold on Francie as he looked up at the other man. "This ain't none of your business, banker man, so go on back inside."

"I'm making it my business." Rick moved closer, wanting to be sure she was unharmed. "Francie, are you all right?"

Paul tightened the grip he had on her arms as he muttered to her in a low voice, "Don't say a word."

"Paul, please, I want to go back inside," she insisted, trying to avoid trouble.

"We're staying here," he countered.

"I said let her go," Rick repeated. He could tell now the man had been drinking, and though he didn't want a fight, he would do what he had to do to get Francie away from the cowhand and keep her safe.

"She's with me. Get lost," Paul snarled. Just to prove his point, he yanked her hard against him and kissed her again.

Francie almost gagged at his hot, disgusting kiss.

Rick saw her trying to resist, and he reacted instantly. Grabbing Francie, he tore her free of the drunken cowboy's grip before taking a swing at the man and knocking him to the ground.

Francie was trembling in fear as Rick went to her.

"Did he hurt you?" he asked, tender concern in his voice.

"No— I— Thank you—"

He put his arm around her shoulders and started to guide her back to the safety of the hall.

Paul had been caught off guard by the banker's attack, but now he was furious. There was no way he was going to let that banker man get away with stealing the girl he wanted. He lurched to his feet, wiping the blood from his mouth as he went after them, determined to take his revenge.

"How did you know I needed you?" Francie was saying as she looked up at Rick with wide-eyed wonder.

Rick smiled down at her, glad that she hadn't been injured in any way. "I was on my way to ask you to dance, but Paul got to you first. I was keeping an eye on you so I could—"

He never got to finish. Paul attacked, launching himself at Rick and shoving Francie forcefully aside.

Shocked by the sudden, unexpected attack, Francie cried out as she fell to the ground.

A few people standing near the door heard her cry and looked outside, trying to see what was going on.

"Fight! There's a fight going on!" one of the men shouted.

Mark had seen Rick follow Paul and Francie outside, so he was pretty sure what was going on.

"That must be Paul—" Mark said to Dusty. Without a thought, he deserted Dusty in the middle of the dance floor and ran outside to see if his friend needed any help.

Dusty looked around and, realizing there was no sign of Francie anywhere inside, she hurried after Mark.

The musicians kept playing, hoping to distract everyone, but a crush of people hurried toward the door.

Dusty found herself trapped behind the crowd, unable to get outside to help her friend.

Meanwhile, outside the hall, Rick was outraged that Paul had so brutally shoved Francie aside, and he feared she might have been injured by the assault. He was holding his own with the drunken ranch hand until Mark joined in, and the two men teamed up on him. When they began to overpower Rick, Francie got up and started to run to the hall to get help, but she didn't get very far. Paul hit Rick savagely, knocking him to the ground and then went after Francie, catching her before she could escape.

"As I recall, this was our dance—" he said, leering down at her and enjoying the look of fear in her eyes as Mark continued the fight with Rick.

"Let her go—"

The unexpected order came out of nowhere.

Paul froze at the sound of the commanding voice. He had no idea who was there, and he looked around in shock as a complete stranger stepped forward from the shadows.

Grant had been on his way to the dance when he'd heard a woman cry out. He'd thought she sounded as if she was in danger, and he had immediately headed in her direction. Now Grant rested his hand on his gun to let the troublemakers know he meant business as he faced them down.

Paul usually wouldn't have listened to anyone ordering him around, but there was something about the stranger's commanding and intimidating presence that stopped him in his tracks. That, and the way the stranger's hand rested so familiarly on his gun. Paul took a step backward, but he didn't release Francie. In fact, his hold on her tightened.

"Maybe you didn't hear me—" Grant repeated threateningly as he moved even closer. "I told you to let her go."

Francie stared up at the stranger in complete surprise. She didn't know who he was, but she was thrilled he'd showed up at this moment. She sensed Paul's sudden uncertainty about the situation, and she took full advantage of it, tearing herself free of his hold and distancing herself from him.

Mark had managed to knock Rick to the ground again, and he looked over in his friend's direction now to see what was going on. He, too, was surprised by the unknown man's interference. He turned on the stranger and thought about going for his own gun, just to show him who was in control of the situation.

"Don't do it," Grant dictated. He'd dealt with this kind before and knew exactly what the other drunk was thinking.

"Who are you?" Paul demanded, still not backing down.

But before Grant could answer him, the crowd that had been watching from the doorway parted, and Grant saw an older man come rushing outside, followed closely by two women.

"What's going on out here?" Fred demanded, rightfully outraged by the sight that greeted him. "Francie?"

She ran to her father as he looked from the two drunken cowboys to the stranger, who had gone to help Rick to his feet.

"Oh, Papa—Paul forced me out here with him and Rick came to help me—" She hurried over to Rick's side as he stood with the other man. "Thank heaven, this gentleman showed up when he did." Francie looked up at the tall, darkly handsome man, wondering who he was. She knew she would have remembered him if she'd seen him before.

Fred turned on Paul, his manner menacing. "Don't you ever go near my daughter again! Do you understand me?"

Paul ignored the older man as he faced the stranger. "I ain't done with you yet, stranger—"

Grant betrayed no emotion as he said calmly and coldly, "Oh, yes, you are."

Paul muttered something vile under his breath. He glared menacingly at the stranger for a moment longer and then stalked off into the night, leaving Mark to follow.

Chapter Seven

Dusty had rushed from the dance hall with Mr. and Mrs. Reynolds, and when she saw that Francie appeared to be in some kind of trouble, her first instinct had been to jump right in and help her friend. She would have, too, had Mrs. Reynolds not caught her by the arm and held her back.

"Stay here— Let the men handle it!" the older woman had ordered.

Only then had Dusty realized that, dressed in a delicate gown as she was, she wouldn't have been much help to Francie. But feeling helpless didn't sit well with her, and she hoped Mr. Reynolds could break up the brawl.

It was as she'd stood back with Mrs. Reynolds that she'd caught sight of the tall, handsome, mysterious man who had seemed to come out of nowhere to help Francie and Rick. She didn't have any idea who he was, but he had certainly been a godsend, showing up to chase off the two drunks.

When Mrs. Reynolds finally released her, Dusty hurried over with Mrs. Reynolds to check on Francie.

*   *   *

Grant stepped back as those who had been watching came rushing over. He looked off in the direction the two drunken cowboys had gone and was glad to see no sign of them lurking nearby in the shadows. Even so, he wasn't sure they were done causing trouble for the night. He'd dealt with their kind many times in the past, and he wanted to make certain they really had heeded his advice and left the area.

It was just as Grant was turning to follow them that he caught sight of the young woman who came rushing over to Francie's side. Tall and slender, she was wearing a fashionable gown with her dark hair styled up and held in place by a fancy bow, and he didn't think he'd ever seen such a pretty girl.

It wasn't often Grant allowed himself to be distracted. He'd learned early on that distractions could be dangerous in his line of work, and this female was definitely a distraction. For just one moment, though, he allowed himself to enjoy the sight of her before forcing himself back to reality.

He had to go to check on the troublemakers—and keep a look out for Jackson and his men.

Grant moved quietly away and disappeared down the street.

The moment of terror past, Francie looked up at Rick as she touched his arm. "Are you all right?"

"I'll live," Rick said in disgust as he wiped some blood off his mouth. He looked around, wanting to thank the man who'd helped him, only to discover that he was gone. "Where did he go?"

"He was right here a minute ago—" Francie said.

Fred joined them along with his wife and Dusty.

"Who was that man?" Fred asked.

"I don't know, but I sure am glad he showed up when he did," Francie said.

"So am I," Rick agreed, disappointed at not getting the chance to speak with him.

"I appreciate your defending my daughter, Rick," Fred said gruffly.

Rick nodded. Normally, he tried to avoid brawling, but he was glad he'd followed Francie outside. There was no telling what Paul might have tried to do to her if he hadn't been there.

"Looks like the excitement's over out here folks," one of the men standing near the door announced. "Let's get some dancing going again."

Those who'd come out to see what all the excitement was about went on back inside to enjoy the rest of the evening.

Mrs. Randolph was still worried as she hovered around her daughter. "Are you sure you weren't hurt, darling?"

"I'm all right, but I would like to freshen up a bit—"

"I'll go with her," Dusty offered.

The two girls started back to the hall, still a little shaken by what had transpired.

Battered though he was, Rick called out to Francie, "Your next dance is mine."

She looked back at him and smiled. "Yes, it is."

Francie and Dusty went in and made their way

to the small, private sitting room that had been put aside for the ladies. They were glad to find there was no one else there when they went in. Francie needed a little privacy to collect herself and to calm down.

"You told me we were going to have an exciting evening, but this wasn't what I thought you had in mind," Dusty told her friend.

"I know—" Francie agreed, starting to tremble a bit as she sat down on the small sofa to compose herself. "I don't even want to think about what might have happened if Rick hadn't come outside when he did—or if that other man hadn't shown up just in time— Do you know him?"

"No. I've never seen him before."

"Neither have I, and it was so strange for him to just appear out of nowhere the way he did. I mean, some of the men in the hall knew the fight was going on, and they didn't do anything—nothing— They just stood there watching. They didn't even try to help Rick— And then that stranger just showed up and faced both Paul and Mark down—"

"There was something about the man—a dangerous edge or— I don't know. And then for him to just disappear the way he did—"

"I wonder where he went?"

"He was probably your guardian angel and he went to make sure those two don't come back to bother you again."

"Oh, I don't know. I think Rick was my guardian angel tonight," Francie said, finally managing a smile as her expression softened.

"That was very brave of him to take on Paul."

"Yes, it was."

"Let's get you freshened up then. Your hero is waiting out there to dance with you."

"I hope Rick's not hurt too bad," Francie said, sounding concerned.

"If he's staying to dance with you, I don't think you have to worry too much about that."

"I just have to worry about the other girls grabbing him," Francie replied with a grin.

"Then hurry up!" Dusty teased.

"All right," Francie said, getting up to check her appearance in the small mirror. "How do I look?"

"Gorgeous! Let's go."

Grant followed in the direction the two drunks had gone, and it didn't take him long to catch sight of them, staggering along up ahead of him. He watched from a distance as they entered the saloon. He hadn't expected them to give up so easily, but he was glad that it seemed they had. He knew the cowhands might drink some more and come back looking for even more trouble, but he hoped they had sense enough to just spend the rest of the night in the saloon, drinking. He had more important things to worry about than a couple of drunken cowboys. He wanted to make sure Les Jackson and his men weren't in town yet, so he had to get back to the dance and take a look around.

Charley was still drinking at the bar when the two hands came in and sat down at a table, yelling for one of the saloon girls to wait on them. There was no missing their conversation as they bragged about the fight they'd just been in at the dance.

"Yeah," one of the men was chuckling to his friend, "I'd say that Randolph girl was worth fighting over, wouldn't you?"

"Especially if you only had to fight that banker for her," the other man answered. "It was too damn bad the other fella showed up when he did. If he hadn't butted in, we mighta had ourselves some real fun tonight."

"Yeah, well, we can have some real fun here with Sassy," the first man said, grabbing the saloon girl as she came to the table and hauling her down on his lap.

"Yes, you can," the girl assured him, leaning forward to give him a big, hungry kiss.

Charley usually didn't pay any attention to what went on there in the saloon, but hearing the news that there had been trouble at the dance, and that it had involved Francie, worried him. Quickly downing the rest of his drink, he left the saloon and hurried back to the hall. He feared Dusty might have gotten caught up in all the ruckus, too, and he grew angry with himself for not being there to make sure she stayed safe and out of harm's way.

His felt a surge of relief when he went back inside and found Dusty dancing with one of the nice young men from town. He was glad to see that she appeared to be enjoying herself, so he went looking for Fred to find out exactly what had happened earlier.

Charley didn't get far, though, before Miss Gertrude saw him coming and cornered him.

"All right, Charley Martin, you've been avoiding me all night, but you're not sneaking past me this time! This is my dance!" she declared, taking his arm.

Even though he'd been drinking, he knew better than to try to get away from Miss Gertrude.

"Yes, ma'am," he responded cordially, "but I have to warn you, it's been quite a while since I've been dancing."

"Once you start moving again, you'll remember how. I saw you with Dusty earlier, and you seemed to be doing just fine," she assured him as they made their way out to the dance floor together. She understood what a rough life Charley had and wanted to try to get a smile out of him. "Your little girl has been behaving herself, in case that's what you're looking so worried about and—" She fixed him with a discerning look. "Just where were you when all the excitement broke out? Down at the saloon?"

"Yes, Miss Gertrude, I'm afraid I was," he admitted. "I didn't think we had to worry about that kind of trouble tonight."

"When these cowhands get all drunked up this way, we always have to worry about there being trouble. Thank heaven Francie wasn't hurt."

"How bad was it?"

"Luckily, the cowboy was interrupted very quickly, but if it hadn't been for our new banker and the stranger who showed up just in time, why, there's no telling what might have happened. It's funny, though—I've been looking around, and I still haven't seen that stranger again. One minute he was there, and the next he'd completely disappeared."

"So some stranger got involved and broke up the fight?"

"You haven't heard the whole story of what happened yet?"

"No, I haven't."

She quickly told him everything. "I don't know who the man was, but I intend to find out. We need more men like him and Rick around these parts—true gentlemen—men of honor. If there were, Canyon Springs would certainly be more civilized."

"Well, if anybody can find out who this stranger was, it'll be you." Charley couldn't help laughing.

"I plan on it," she declared, and she kept an eye out for any sign of the man as she and Charley finished their dance and moved apart.

When Grant returned to the hall, he was glad to find that the dance seemed to be back to normal. He knew the festive atmosphere would make it easier for him to just blend in with those in attendance and keep a lookout for Jackson and his men at the same time.

What he didn't know was that the eagle-eyed Miss Gertrude was keeping a lookout for him.

At that particular moment, the music paused to signal the end of a dance.

Miss Gertrude was making her way back to her seat when the announcement came for the much-anticipated second "ladies' choice" dance. Everyone was excited, and Miss Gertrude turned and swept the room with a sharp-eyed gaze. It was then that she caught sight of the stranger at the far end of the hall. Tall, lean, broad-shouldered and real good-looking, the new man in town stood out in the crowd, and Miss Gertrude was ready for him.

Grant saw the prim elderly lady making her determined way through the crowd. He thought nothing of it—at first. Only when she came straight up to him and took him by the hand was he surprised.

"I've been looking for you, young man," Miss Gertrude said, giving him a conspiratorial grin as she boldly drew him out onto the dance floor.

"You have?" He looked down at her as he took her in his arms to dance, and it was then he saw the unmistakable twinkle of mischief in her eyes and knew she was a woman to deal with.

"I saw what you did outside, breaking up the fight that way, and I wanted to thank you for helping out. Did you go follow those two troublemakers to make sure they weren't coming back?"

"Yes, ma'am, I did."

"That was smart of you," she said, nodding her approval. "Paul and Mark are known for not being the brightest boys around, and they do like stirring things up and causing a lot of trouble. It makes them feel like real big men."

"Last I saw of them, they were going into the saloon."

"That's the best place for them. I hope they stay there," she told him with satisfaction.

"With any luck, they will," he agreed with her.

"Well, in case no one's told you—you're quite a fine dancer, young man."

"Why, thank you."

"No need to thank me. I only tell the truth." Miss Gertrude smiled up at him. "I'm Gertrude Stevens, by the way. What's your name?"

"I'm Grant Spencer."

"I am pleased to meet you, Grant Spencer."

"I'm pleased to meet you, too, Miss Stevens."

"Everybody calls me Miss Gertrude. I expect you to do the same," she stated in her usual manner.

"Yes, ma'am, Miss Gertrude," he quickly complied.

"I haven't seen you around here before, have I?"

"No, ma'am. I just rode into town tonight."

"Are you planning on staying for a while?" she asked hopefully.

"No, I'm just passing through."

"That's too bad. I could get used to dancing with you at all the socials," she teased, and her flirtatious remark got a smile out of him. She'd known he was handsome before, but when he smiled down at her, her heart actually skipped a beat. Miss Gertrude found herself wishing she was twenty again. If she had been, he would have been in trouble.

"And I could get used to dancing with you," he returned.

Miss Gertrude laughed good-naturedly. "You're a charmer, that's for sure. Welcome to Canyon Springs, Grant. I hope you have a good time while you are here."

"I already am," he said, enjoying her company. It

had been a long time since he'd been with anyone like Miss Gertrude. He knew ladies like her were rare. "I'm with you."

"Ladies! It's that time! Are you ready? Change partners!"

Gertrude had known the announcement would be coming, and she was sorry to hear it. There was something about this young man that intrigued her. She wanted to find out more about him, but as much as she would have liked to hang on to him, she knew she had to give him up. Luckily, she glanced around and was glad to see that Dusty was nearby, dancing with one of the local ranch hands.

"I know just who to give you to," she said.

"You do?" He had no idea what Miss Gertrude was up to.

"That's right."

She took him by the hand and quickly guided him over to Dusty.

"Here you are, honey. Grant is all yours."

Chapter Eight

Gertrude saw the look of surprised delight on Dusty's face as she turned around to dance with her new partner and came face-to-face with Grant. Gertrude smiled to herself as she snared Dusty's former partner and allowed herself to be danced away.

Dusty had been so busy dancing, she hadn't seen the stranger return to the hall, and she certainly hadn't seen Miss Gertrude claim him for the ladies' choice dance. She gazed up at the tall, handsome man, stunned for a moment.

Grant, too, was amazed by this unexpected turn of events. He'd deliberately put aside all thoughts of this woman when he'd followed the two drunks from the scene of the fight. He'd known she was a beauty, but he'd also known he didn't have time for a woman in his life. Certainly not now, and there were times when he was beginning to wonder if he ever would. But here he was, staring down at the slender, dark-haired beauty as she came oh-so-willingly into his arms.

"Shall we?" he invited.

"Let's—" she answered a bit breathlessly as he began to guide her gracefully about the dance floor.

"I'm Grant, by the way," he told her.

"And I'm—" For just an instant, she paused and then said, "Justine."

For this one dance—

For this one moment in time—

She wanted to live the fantasy and be the girl she appeared to be tonight—

"It's nice to meet you, Justine." He'd noticed her momentary hesitation introducing herself, but thought she was just shy.

"It's nice to meet you, too. I'm sure Miss Gertrude already thanked you for your help, but I want to thank you, too, for stopping the fight. It seemed no one else cared—they were all just standing around watching."

"I was glad to help. It's good no one was seriously hurt."

"I told Francie I thought you were her guardian angel, showing up out of nowhere like you did."

Grant chuckled. "I've been called many things in my time, but never a guardian angel."

"Well, there's a first time for everything," she told him with a smile. She certainly felt as if she was in heaven there in his arms.

They fell silent as they continued to dance.

Grant forced himself to lift his gaze away from the stunning beauty in his arms and look around the hall once more. He had to be vigilant. He had to keep watch. He didn't think Jackson and his boys would know him on sight, but he couldn't be sure, and he would take no chances where they were concerned. They were cold-blooded killers. He knew that given the choice, they would just as soon shoot someone as let them go. That was why he was after the outlaws, and he wouldn't rest until their days of robbing and killing were over.

Dusty wanted the dance to go on forever, but she knew it couldn't last, so she savored every minute. She looked up at Grant.

"Will you be here in town long?"

"No, I'm just passing through," he answered.

"That's too bad," she remarked.

He surprised himself when he answered, "Yes, it is."

They were about to say more when the announcement came again to switch partners.

Before Grant could say another word, one of the men nearby grabbed the dark-haired beauty and danced off with her, leaving him to take up the other man's abandoned partner. He kept smiling and was cordial, but, in truth, he was waiting for the dance to end. He needed to take another close look around town.

And Grant did just that.

When the ladies' choice finally ended, he checked the room once more. He saw no sign of Jackson or his men. He did see Justine being escorted back to the far side of the hall by her last dancing partner. He was tempted to go speak with her again, but denied himself. A sense of regret came over him for a moment, but he managed to ignore it.

He had a job to do.

With long, determined strides, Grant left the hall.

As the next dance started up, Dusty looked around and was thoroughly disappointed when she saw no sign of Grant anywhere. In her fantasy, she'd imagined him hurrying across the dance floor to take her in his arms again. But it wasn't going to happen. It was just that—a fantasy. Grant was gone.

It wasn't much later when her father sought her out.

"If we're going to be heading out at sunup, it's time for us to call it a night," Charley told her.

"I know." She realized now she probably would never see the handsome stranger again.

"Did you have a good time?" He'd been watching her and had noticed that she'd looked especially happy this evening.

"Yes—except for the fight. If I hadn't been dressed like this, I might have been more help to Francie."

"Everything looks like it turned out all right."

Dusty knew that was true, for she'd seen her friend dancing with Rick several times that evening.

They sought out Francie and her parents to let them know they had to leave, and Fred accompanied them back to his house to get Dusty's personal belongings before father and daughter returned home.

When they got to their own house, Dusty bid her father good night and went on to her bedroom.

The effects of the liquor he'd consumed had worn off, and Charley was sober now as he watched her go down the hall. He was deeply thankful that nothing had happened to Dusty while he'd been at the saloon. He knew from now on he would put her safety above all else in his life. He went to bed, too, knowing morning would be coming all too soon.

Dusty sat down at her small, plain dressing table and started to take the ribbon from her hair. She paused for a moment to stare at her own reflection, seeing the girl she'd been for just that night. In all these months of riding the stage with her father, she'd become so accustomed to being known as "the kid" that she'd almost completely forgotten what it felt like to be a girl. She had enjoyed her time at the dance tonight, and she had enjoyed those few moments of being "Justine" with the stranger named Grant.

Sighing, Dusty pulled the ribbon from her hair and took off the jewelry Francie had loaned her. She made short order of slipping out of the dress and quickly changed into her nightgown. She washed her face and brushed out her hair and happened to cast one last glance in the mirror as she started to climb into bed. The change was startling. This time it was Dusty who stared back at her, not Justine.

For one moment, she allowed herself to wonder what Grant would think of her if he saw her now, and then she put the thought from her. No man would be interested in her when she looked like this.

No, she was Dusty Martin—Charley's "kid," who rode shotgun on the stage.

This was who she really was.

This was her life now. The fun tonight had been just an escape for a few hours. Reality would return with the dawn.

Tomorrow morning, she would be back in her work clothes, wearing her gun belt and carrying her shotgun.

Dusty put out the lamp on the bedside table and went to bed. She needed to get some sleep if she was going to be ready to ride in the morning. As she drifted off, she found herself wondering if she would ever see Grant again.

Grant was cautious as he made his way around town. He not only had to keep a lookout for Jackson and his men, but now, he also had the two drunks from the dance to consider.

He'd stopped by the saloon for one more drink and was glad to find that the two drunken ranch hands who'd caused the trouble earlier were gone. He had bigger things to worry about than those two. Satisfied that he'd beaten Jackson and his men to town, he finished off his whiskey. Several of the saloon girls approached him, but he had no interest in what they were offering. Instead, he left the saloon and went back to the hotel to bed down for the night.

After lighting the small lamp on the bedside table, Grant unbuckled his gun belt and put it within easy reach. Stopping at the window, he pushed the curtain aside to look down at the night-shrouded street below. The town was quiet and peaceful, and

he wondered how long it was going to stay that way
with the outlaw gang due to ride in at any time.

Grant knew there was nothing he could do but
wait, so he got undressed and stretched out on the
bed. He turned off the lamp and lay staring up at
the ceiling. He wondered if he would see Justine
around town again, and then warned himself
against such thoughts. The innocent beauty had
been a temptation, but a girl like her didn't fit his
lifestyle. He closed his eyes and sought what rest
he could find.

Dusty was up and dressed before dawn. Matt Collins, the extra guard her father had hired for the
trip, planned to meet them at the office early that
morning, so she knew she had to be ready to go.
They collected the personal belongings they needed
and left the house, ready to go to work.

They reached the stage office to find Hank there
waiting for them along with Matt. The team had
already been hitched and now it was just a matter
of waiting for the passengers to show up. They were
taking three men on this run.

"Dusty will ride in the stage with the passengers. Matt, I want you to ride up on the bench with
me," Charley directed.

"I'll keep my shotgun with me, just in case,"
Dusty told Matt. "Let's just hope I don't need it."

"You're right," Matt agreed.

Dusty wasn't really looking forward to this trip.
The long, tedious hours of riding in the close con-
fines of the stagecoach with three men who were

strangers to her wouldn't be easy, but she would do it. She was used to riding up on the bench with her father, but because of the payroll, this was necessary.

It wasn't long before the passengers arrived. Dusty eyed the men quickly and then set about stowing their bags while they climbed into the stage. When she was done, she got in with them and sat down next to the man who appeared to be from back East, since he was traveling in a suit.

Charley came to speak with the men as Dusty settled in. "My kid, Dusty, here, is going to be riding with you." He handed her the shotgun.

"Are you expecting trouble?" asked the man sitting next to Dusty, nervously looking at the shotgun.

"We always expect trouble," her father answered. "It's safer for us that way. It's better not to be surprised."

Charley closed the stagecoach door and climbed up to the driver's bench, where Matt was already seated and waiting for him.

They were ready to roll.

Inside the stage, the Easterner continued to stare at Dusty. He was more than a little uncomfortable. The shotgun was a good-size weapon, and he thought the driver's son was hardly old enough to handle such a dangerous gun.

"Do you know how to use that shotgun?" he asked.

Dusty looked over at him and nodded. "Yes, sir, I do."

The Easterner swallowed nervously and scooted as far over in the seat as he could. He wanted to put as much room between them as he could.

Dusty realized he was intimidated and she smiled slightly. The farther he stayed away from her, the better. She directed her attention out the stage window as the stage drove out of town. Even though she wasn't up riding with her father, it was her job to be alert and watch for trouble—especially on this run.

The Following Night

The sun had set and darkness covered the land as the outlaw gang relaxed around the campfire, sharing a bottle of whiskey.

"It won't be long now, boys," Les Jackson said with a grin as he took a deep swig of the potent liquor. "Tomorrow is our big day. Once we get that payroll, we can do some real celebrating."

"And I'm looking forward to it." Ugly Joe Williams grabbed the whiskey bottle from Les. With his broken, bulbous nose and mostly toothless smile, the nickname fit him perfectly. "Them saloon girlies will be chasing me all over once they see how much money I got."

"You gonna make them chase you for very long?" Cale Pierce asked.

"No! Whichever one of them gets to me first is going to earn herself a whole lot of money!"

"I didn't think you'd hold out," Cale taunted.

They all laughed.

"How early are we going to ride out?" Ugly Joe asked Les.

"At sunup. We have to be at the pass early."

They had worked out their plan for robbing the stage very carefully and believed they would have no trouble pulling it off.

"I wonder what happened to Jim?" Cale remarked.

"I don't know. It ain't like him not to show up." Ugly Joe was worried about the other gunman. With the law after them, they'd split up several days earlier and arranged to meet outside Canyon Springs. Now, Jim was the only one missing, and the other men were troubled by his absence.

"If he can get here, he will," Les added.

"It'd be a shame if he missed out on this robbery," Cale put in.

The other outlaws nodded as they thought about the robbery they had planned. Cale had been in the saloon in Canyon Springs when the stage driver had gotten drunk and mentioned transporting the payroll. Cale had immediately sought out Les to let him know what he'd learned. Now, after meeting up with Ugly Joe, they were ready to pull off the robbery. There was a payroll on that stage and they were going to make it theirs. It was just too bad that Jim hadn't caught up with them yet.

"Well, if he doesn't show up, that'll just mean more money for each of us!" Ugly Joe chuckled. Even as he said it, though, he knew they could use the extra gun riding with them.

"If Jim doesn't show up, that'll mean he's dead," Les said grimly. He didn't like thinking that way, but he knew he had to consider the possibility. After all, the Rangers were tracking the gang.

They all went back to drinking, not wanting to believe the worst could have happened to their friend, and hoping that if the law had caught up with Jim, he hadn't revealed any of their plans. They certainly didn't want to find Texas Rangers, ready and waiting for them when they robbed the stage.

Chapter Nine

Dusty was exhausted when they reached the way station the second night out. The day had been a long one. The trip had been uneventful so far, and that was good, but the heat had been stifling and the ride in the cramped stagecoach had been bone jarring.

The one thing that had kept her spirits up over the many miles they'd traveled was the memory of her dance with the handsome stranger in town. She allowed herself to fantasize about wearing the fancy gown and being in his arms, for it helped distract her from the reality of being jammed in the stagecoach with several fat, sweaty, smelly passengers. She was so tired now, though, the snoring of the men bedded down around her in the one big sleeping room didn't bother her at all. She fell asleep quickly and slept soundly all night long. When she awoke just before dawn, she realized her father was already up and moving, so she got up and went to help him.

The wife of the man who ran the way station was a fine cook, and by the time Dusty and her father came back inside, she had already started making breakfast for the passengers. Dusty was eagerly looking forward to the meal. The food at this way station was always delicious fare. Everyone ate hungrily, knowing it was going to be another long day of travel.

When they'd finished their meal, Charley, Matt and Dusty went out to get the stagecoach ready.

"All right, let's get a move on!" Charley called when they were loaded up.

As had become their custom, the men climbed in first. Dusty stood with her father and Matt near the team so the passengers couldn't hear their conversation.

"We'll reach the pass about noon," Charley said, frowning. "You two, be ready. If anybody's going to try anything, that'll be the place."

"We'll be watching," Matt assured him.

Dusty joined the men in the stagecoach, carrying her shotgun, while Matt and Charley settled in on the driver's bench. Even this early in the morning, the heat was sweltering, and Dusty could tell as they pulled out of the way station that it was going to be another tough day.

Les, Cale and Ugly Joe were up at the crack of dawn and riding out. When they reached the pass, they took a careful look around to make sure there was no one else in the area.

"Where do you want us to be waiting for them?" Ugly Joe asked. He figured they'd just take up positions on both sides of the pass and shoot the driver and the man riding shotgun when they drove through. He knew it would be a little tricky catching up with the stage afterward, for the team would be running wild, but all that mattered to him was getting his hands on the money. He didn't care about what happened to any passengers.

"All right, boys, this is what we're going to do," Les directed, looking up at the steep, craggy hillside. "We're gonna push some of those rocks down here and block the road, so the stage will have to stop when it comes through."

"That's real smart, Les," Ugly Joe said, impressed by his plan. That would definitely make the robbery simpler for them.

"Once they stop to move the rocks, it'll be easy pickin's for us," Cale agreed.

"It should be, but don't forget, some of the passengers might be carrying guns, too. Don't go thinking this is going to be too easy," Les warned them. He knew there was always a chance for trouble.

"You're right, Les. This ain't no time to be getting careless," Ugly Joe said.

"All right, let's get this done," Les ordered. "The stage should be passing through within the next hour."

Cale and Ugly Joe tempered their jubilant moods and set about climbing up the hillside to roll down the biggest rocks they could move. They had to make sure it looked like a natural landslide, so the stage driver wouldn't immediately suspect anything.

Charley was tense as the road narrowed and they headed up into the pass.

"The sooner we get through here, the better," he told Matt as he kept careful control of the team. "Be ready—"

"I am."

They hadn't gone too much farther and had just started around a curve when Charley caught sight of what appeared to be a rock slide on the trail ahead. He swore loudly as he fought to slow the horses.

Dusty realized her father was forcefully reining in the team, and she leaned out the window to yell up to him, "What's wrong?"

"There're some rocks in the road!" he shouted back as he brought the stagecoach to a halt.

"What is it?" the Easterner asked, looking worried.

"Looks like we're going to have to stop and clear some rocks out of the road," Dusty explained as she threw open the stagecoach door and climbed down. She made sure to keep her shotgun with her.

Charley looked over at Matt. "You stay here. I'll get the other men to help me." He jumped down and went to speak to the passengers. "Come on, you boys, I need some help." Glancing over at Dusty, he ordered, "You keep an eye on the stagecoach with Matt."

Charley took a quick look around, but didn't see anything else that seemed out of the ordinary. As the three passengers joined him, they started to roll the bigger rocks out of the way.

"Good thing you saw the rocks in time," one of the men said. He realized how much damage could have been done to the stage if it had run into the boulders. They might have been stuck out there for a day or two, making repairs.

"Charley ain't called the best driver around these parts for nothing," Matt assured them.

Spread out above them, hiding among the rocks, Les, Ugly Joe and Cale were watching and waiting for the right time to make their move. So far, their scheme was working out just the way they'd planned. It didn't often happen this way, and Les was feeling confident.

He kept an eye on the man riding shotgun and on the boy who'd gotten out of the stage carrying another shotgun. The presence of the extra gun convinced Les even more that the payroll was on this stage.

Les had seen three more men get out of the stagecoach. He'd watched as they seemed to look nervously around and then went to help the driver clear the road. Once they'd started to work, he gave Ugly Joe and Cale the signal.

It was time.

Dusty was standing guard, scanning the steep hillside, watching for trouble. The only warning she had was the glint of the sun off the barrel of one of the outlaws' rifles. She raised her gun to get off a shot in that direction as she yelled to warn her father, "Papa! There's—"

Startled by her frantic call as she fired her shotgun, Matt and her father both looked her way, but before they could react it was too late.

Accurate and deadly gunfire rained down upon them.

Matt was killed instantly where he was sitting atop the stagecoach, and Dusty was shot, grazed by a bullet that knocked her backward among the rocks alongside the trail.

"Dusty!" Charley yelled in horror. He went for his own gun.

Les and Ugly Joe got off several more rounds and watched in satisfaction as the stage driver fell and lay unmoving in the dirt. Then they turned their attention to the three men who had run for cover.

"Come out with your hands up and we'll let you live!" Les shouted down to the passengers.

The Easterner and the two other men knew they were trapped. They had no way to escape. One of the men was armed, but he knew he was no match for these killers. He tossed his gun out where the outlaws could see it.

"There's my gun!"

"All right— Now come out real slowlike—"

"We're coming out!"

The three men came to stand in the middle of the road.

"Cale— You stay up here. If any one of them makes a move, shoot him," Les told him as he and Ugly Joe started down to tie up the three men and get the strongbox.

The three passengers knew they were dealing with cold-blooded killers. They offered no resistance as the two outlaws shoved them to the ground and tied their hands behind their backs. Ugly Joe made short order of taking their wallets and other valuables. The Easterner tried to protest, and Ugly Joe hit him upside the head with his gun, knocking him unconscious. He then went to take what money the driver and the two guards had on them.

Les wasted no time climbing up on the stage and hauling out the strongbox. He threw it down on the ground and climbed down to shoot the lock off. He threw it open. "Yee-ha, boys! We're getting paid real good today!"

He started to stuff all the cash into the saddlebags he'd brought along, excited by the haul they'd made.

Ugly Joe took what little money the driver and the one dead guard had on him and then headed over to check the other guard. He knelt down and grabbed the younger, smaller guard, turning him over. There was blood on the boy's forehead, and when the kid gave a low groan, Ugly Joe realized that he wasn't dead.

Ugly Joe grabbed up the kid's gun and tossed it far away, just in case. As he began to search the skinny kid's pockets for money, he made a big discovery. He looked up at Les in shock.

"Les— Get over here!"

"What is it?" Les asked, irritated. He didn't want to waste any time. They needed to pack up the cash and get out of there. They needed to put some long miles between them and the scene of the robbery.

"I ain't never in all my days seen anything like this—"

"Like what? He's still alive?"

"Yeah, the bullet just grazed him, but—"

"But what?"

"This ain't no 'him.' "

"What are you talking about?"

"This here guard is a girl!"

"A girl?"

Les finished stowing all the money and then went over to see what Ugly Joe was talking about.

Just as Les joined the other outlaw, Dusty began to regain consciousness. She gave another groan as she struggled to open her eyes. She could hear the men's voices and thought it was her father talking with some of the other men on the stage.

"Papa—? What happened?" She finally managed to look up, and only then did she realize it was the outlaw's hands upon her. The shock and horror of the attack returned with a vengeance and she tried to throw herself violently away from him.

Her weak effort proved futile. His hold on her was powerful. He wasn't about to let her go.

"Don't go trying anything, little honey. I'd hate for you to get hurt any worse than you already are," Ugly Joe said, leering down at her.

Les was still shocked by Ugly Joe's discovery. He'd thought it strange enough that the stage driver would have a kid riding shotgun for him, but he was astonished to find out the guard was a girl.

"Let me go!" Dusty continued to try to get away, but it was impossible.

"You're not going anywhere," Les finally ground out. "Tie her up and get her ready to ride."

"What are we going to do with her?" Ugly Joe couldn't imagine what Les had in mind.

"You'll see," Les said, already making his plan.

"But she's only going to slow us down."

"Don't go questioning my orders," Les raged at him. "Just do as I say!"

Les left Ugly Joe to take care of the girl and went to turn the team loose. The longer it took for the holdup to be reported, the bigger head start the outlaws would have on any posse that tried to come after them.

Ugly Joe got up and pulled the girl to her feet. He tied her hands in front of her as she stood swaying weakly in front of him.

As they were finishing up, Cale rode down, leading their horses.

"Let's get out of here," Les directed. "I'll keep the girl with me."

Cale was surprised to find out about the guard's identity. "You're taking her along?"

"Like I told Ugly Joe, I got a plan. So don't you go worrying about it. Let's ride."

Les loaded up the saddlebags and started to drag the girl over to his horse.

Dusty was in agony. The pain in her head was nearly unbearable. She was having trouble trying to concentrate on what was happening around her as the outlaw forced her along with him to his horse.

It was then that she saw her father's body and heart-wrenching agony tore through her. "My father— *You killed my father—*"

"Shut up," Les snarled, "unless you want me to shoot the other three."

Dusty fell silent in her terror. The man's grip on her was harsh, and she realized there was no escape. The outlaw leader shoved her up on his horse and then mounted behind her.

"Let's ride, boys! We got some miles to cover!" Les was feeling real good as he rode off, leaving Ugly Joe and Cale to follow.

Chapter Ten

With what little strength she had, Dusty held on tight as they raced away from the site of the robbery. Dark despair filled her. Unless the passengers managed to somehow get loose, she knew it would be long hours before anyone even discovered the stage had been robbed and her father and Matt killed. She thought about trying to throw herself from the horse's back, but the outlaw had both arms around her, so there would be no getting away. In silent agony, she grieved over her father's death.

Les led the way as they covered the long miles. He figured they would have close to a full day's head start on any posse that came after them, so he was feeling confident they would get clean away. When they stopped for the first time to water the horses, he dismounted and then reached up to drag the girl down out of the saddle.

"Don't even think about trying anything," he warned.

Dusty looked around and knew there was no possibility of escape right now, so she quietly went

down to the water to get a drink and to wash some
of the dried blood from her face. It wasn't easy
with her hands tied, but she did her best.

Ugly Joe was eyeing their prisoner as he walked
over to Les. She didn't look like much of a female.
"So, why did you bring her along, Les?"

"I already told you—don't you go worrying about
my plans for her."

"She will slow us down," Cale put in, repeating
Ugly Joe's concern.

"She ain't slowed us down yet, has she?" Les
countered angrily.

"You ain't got no place to keep her," Ugly Joe
said.

"You're right. I don't. I didn't bring her along for
me. She's part of the loot we just robbed from the
stage."

"What are you talking about?" Cale asked.

"Eduardo at the cantina is looking for some new
girls. He told me he'd pay real good if I brought
him some down—especially if they were virgins."

"So you ain't planning on sharing her with us?"
Cale asked. He'd thought at least they were going
to have their fun with the little gal.

"Oh, no. She's worth a lot of money, and I plan
to collect it." Les was smiling at the thought. "Now,
let's ride. We got more important things to worry
about. Like making sure there are no Rangers on
our tail."

They mounted up and rode out again, not stopping for the night until it was almost dark. They

built a small campfire, and Les forced Dusty to sit beside him there. Cale dug out the dried meat they'd brought along, and Les took some from him and held it out to her.

"Eat."

Dusty looked up at him, all the hatred she was feeling for her captor burning in her eyes. "No," she said defiantly.

Les had expected as much, and he smiled coldly at her. "You'll eat this or I'll shove it down your throat—and I don't think you want me to do that." His expression turned menacing.

Dusty had no doubt the outlaw would do exactly what he threatened. She also knew that if she wanted to have any hope of escaping, she needed to eat to keep her strength up. It was hard enough dealing with the pain and dizziness she was suffering. In disgust, she took the offered meat from him and ate it quickly. After they'd finished the food, Les got up and came back with his rope. He sat back down near her.

"Stick your arms out," he ordered.

Les quickly tied the rope to the length that he'd already used to bind her wrists. He tied the other end to his own arm.

"I want to make sure you stay nice and close to me all night." The rope was long enough for her to take care of her needs without his having to stand over her, but if she tried to get away in the middle of the night, he'd know.

Ugly Joe was chuckling as he got his bottle of whiskey out of his saddlebags and took a deep drink.

"Yes, sir, things couldn't have turned out any better today. We did real good. I feel like doing some celebrating."

"I'm with you on that," Cale agreed, grabbing the bottle from Ugly Joe when he held it out. He took a swallow and passed it on to their leader. "Here, Les."

Les enjoyed a drink and handed it back to Ugly Joe. "That's some good whiskey, but don't go drinking too much. We have to ride out at sunup."

They grumbled at his order, but knew he was right.

"Do you think Jim's going to be able find us?" Ugly Joe wondered.

"It's hard to say," Les answered.

"We were lucky we didn't need the extra gun today."

"Yeah, but with him not being here, that's more money for us!" Ugly Joe grinned greedily at the thought.

"Right," Cale agreed. He was going to enjoy doing some serious gambling as soon as he got the chance. He knew it was going to be a while, though. He and his buddies had to make sure the law wasn't closing in on them before they could really let themselves relax and have a good time.

Les tossed a small blanket at Dusty as he got ready to bed down close by. "Cale, you keep first watch."

The other gunman moved away from the fire to sit in the darkness and keep a lookout for trouble. Les didn't think there was any posse close by, but it was better to post a guard and be sure.

Dusty wrapped herself in the blanket and sought what comfort she could find on the hard ground. Sadness and fear overwhelmed her, and she began to cry. She fought to stifle the sobs that wracked her as she thought of her father and Matt. She supposed she ought to be grateful to be alive, but she wondered how fortunate she really was. She had overheard what the outlaw leader had planned for her, and she wondered what new horrors awaited her. In the darkness of the night, she began to pray desperately, begging for help and the strength to get through this.

At dawn, the outlaws were up and riding out. They wouldn't rest again until nightfall.

Canyon Springs

Grant slept later than usual that morning. He had stayed at the saloon late the night before, drinking and gambling a bit to fit in, and hoping to learn something about the outlaws, but he hadn't heard a thing. His mood was tense as he got up and dressed. He wasn't a man used to waiting for trouble. Trouble usually found him, and just sitting there in Canyon Springs waiting for Les and his boys to show up was testing his patience. He knew the information he'd received about their meeting place had been reliable. He told himself to relax, that the outlaws would eventually show up.

Grant left the hotel and headed over to the general store to get the supplies he was going to need when he did finally ride out. As he was about

a block away from the store, he noticed a young boy
rush out of the place and run on down the street to
the stable. The boy seemed to be frantic about
something, and Grant wondered what was going
on. He found out as soon as he stepped through the
door.

"I can't believe it!" exclaimed Alice Jones, the
clerk at the store, her expression horrified as she
spoke with the other ladies who were there.

"It can't be— It just can't be—"

Grant recognized the voice of the little lady who
was standing with her back to him. It was Miss Gertrude. He could hear the heartbreak in her voice
and wondered what had happened. He immediately
went to her side.

"Miss Gertrude— Is something wrong?" he
asked, seeing the tears in her eyes as she looked
up at him.

"Oh, Grant— I didn't know you were still in
town. Somehow, you always do manage to show up
at the right time—" she said in a choked voice.

He couldn't help himself. He put a protective
arm around her shoulders as he looked at the two
other women standing there with her. "What happened?"

"The stage was robbed and Charley Martin and
the man riding shotgun were both killed—" Alice
began.

Grant tensed at the news.

"The telegram came in just a short while ago—"
Betty added.

Miss Gertrude touched his arm as she explained the rest. "And they've kidnapped Dusty—"

"Dusty?" Grant frowned, not recognizing the name.

"She didn't tell you?" Miss Gertrude realized that Dusty must have kept her other life hidden from him the night of the dance. "Justine's nickname is Dusty."

Grant's expression hardened. "She was on the stagecoach?"

Miss Gertrude quickly explained the truth of Dusty's life to him. "It's been hard for her since her mother died, riding shotgun on the stage with her father, but she did it and he was proud of her. And now—"

He couldn't imagine the beauty he'd danced with in the hands of an outlaw gang. "Where did the holdup take place?"

"At the pass," Betty said. "From what the boy was telling us, they think it was that notorious Jackson gang."

Grant grew furious. While he'd been waiting for the outlaws to show up in town, they'd managed to pull off a deadly robbery and take the girl with them.

"We have to let Fred know," Alice put in, knowing her boss and his family needed to know what had happened.

"This is going to break Francie's little heart." Miss Gertrude looked even more miserable at the news.

Betty went on, "Supposedly, the sheriff's going to get a posse together, but the outlaws already have a full day's head start on them—"

"Sheriff Perkins is useless," Miss Gertrude declared. "He'll never be able to find Dusty, not after all this time. Why, he couldn't find his own way home if he didn't have directions. He'll never be able to track them down—"

"Now, Miss Gertrude," Alice scolded.

"Don't 'Now, Miss Gertrude' me," she countered angrily. "I can't tell you how many times he's gone after some troublemaker and come back empty-handed."

"If you ladies will excuse me," Grant said, leaving abruptly.

Miss Gertrude watched him stride purposefully from the store.

"I wonder why he left like that," Alice said.

"I don't know, but I intend to find out," Miss Gertrude told her as she hurried after him.

Betty looked at Alice. "Poor Dusty."

"I hope they can find her and bring her back."

"I do, too."

"One of us should go tell Francie and her family what's happened."

"I'll go," Betty offered, knowing it was going to be a difficult conversation.

Grant was headed straight back to the hotel. He wasn't going to bother with talking to the local lawman. From what Miss Gertrude had said, it would be a waste of his time, and he'd already done enough of that.

"Grant— Wait—" Miss Gertrude called out. She'd thought he might be going over to help the sheriff, but it looked as if he was going to the hotel.

He stopped at her call and waited respectfully for her to catch up with him.

"Where are you going? The sheriff's office is the other way," she pointed out. She'd always sensed that this man was something more than just a drifter passing through town, and she had a feeling she was about to find out his real purpose in coming to Canyon Springs.

"If the sheriff's as bad at tracking as you say he is, I'm not waiting for him." Grant reached in his pocket and took out his badge to pin it on.

Gertrude's eyes widened as she gazed up at him. "You're a Ranger—"

"Yes, ma'am, and I'm going after Les Jackson."

A look of pride came into her eyes as she saw his fierce determination. "I knew there was something special about you from the first time I laid eyes on you." She took him by the arm and pulled him down to her so she could kiss his cheek. "Find Dusty, Grant. Bring her back home."

"I will," he promised her.

With that, he strode off toward the hotel to get his belongings.

He'd lost enough time already.

Less than twenty minutes later, Grant rode out of Canyon Springs.

Over an hour later, Francie was still in her mother's arms, crying hysterically as her father packed his saddlebags getting ready to ride out of town with the posse.

"We're going to need your prayers," Fred told his wife and daughter. "With the big lead they've got on us, I don't know if we'll be able to find them or not."

Francie lifted her head to look at her father. "You have to find her, Papa! You have to!" She left her mother's embrace and went to hug her father. "Please, please tell me you're going to find her!"

Fred held her to his heart as he wrapped his arms around her. "I'm going to do my best, Francie. If we can find her, we will."

"Who all is riding with you?" Marlene asked.

"So far, I've heard that Rick will join us, and several of the businessmen from town. I think some of the ranchers are even sending a few of their hands to help us, so we should have enough guns in case we do manage to catch up with the Jackson gang. It's just taking Sheriff Perkins so long to put the posse together. Every minute counts right now, and the sheriff is slow—"

"I know," Francie said in an emotion-choked voice. "I wish I could ride with you and help."

"No, darling," her father said seriously, "you stay right here with your mother, so I know you're safe." He lifted his gaze to look at his wife. "I'd better get back over to the jail. There's no telling what time we'll be riding out."

Marlene went into his arms to give him a kiss. Fred gave Francie a fatherly hug and then grabbed up his rifle and saddlebags and left the house to mount up and ride away.

Francie stood in the doorway with her mother, fighting desperately to control her tears as she watched her father leave. "They have to find her, Mother— They have to! Who knows what those outlaws might do to Dusty!"

Marlene understood her daughter's fear for her friend. She felt the same way. Dusty was a gentle, caring young woman who had been through some real hard times in her life. It seemed so unfair that tragedy had struck again—Marlene was sickened by the thought.

"The best thing we can do is to pray for Dusty. We'll pray that she is safe and that the posse can track the gang down and rescue her."

Francie looked up at her mother, knowing she was right. "She's got to come back—"

Marlene hugged her daughter again and offered up a silent prayer for Dusty's safety.

When Fred reached the jail, he found Sheriff Perkins standing out in front with about nine other men, including Rick. They had their horses and their gear, and they looked like they were ready to ride.

"Perkins, when are we leaving?" Fred demanded. "Every minute counts right now! They killed Charley and Matt and they've kidnapped Dusty!"

Sheriff Perkins, an arrogant, black-haired, mustachioed man, looked over at him and sneered, "We're leaving when I'm good and ready."

A rumble went through the gathered men.

"Don't you go giving me any trouble, boys. I'm the law in this town."

They fell silent, all thinking that Canyon Springs could use a better man.

"Sheriff, we respect that, but they've taken Dusty," Rick said, stepping up. "We've got to get her back."

Fred went to stand with the young banker. He had come to respect Rick in the short time he'd been there in town. "Rick's right, Sheriff. Dusty needs us."

Sheriff Perkins was agitated, and seriously afraid of giving chase to the deadly gang. He knew Les and his men were likely to kill their pursuers on sight, and he was in no hurry to die. He liked his job there in quiet little Canyon Springs. There wasn't much more trouble than a couple of drunks fighting every now and then, and he could handle that pretty easily. The Jackson gang, though, had him terrified, and he was fighting hard not to let his fear show in front of the other men. If he wanted to keep his job, he had to play the role.

"All right, fellas, Fred's here now. Let's go find these killers!"

Rick and Fred exchanged troubled looks as they went to mount up. They knew it was going to be hard work tracking the outlaws when they had such a big lead, but they were determined to do everything in their power to bring Dusty home.

Chapter Eleven

Dusty had always considered herself to be a strong person, especially after the long months spent riding shotgun with her father. She'd come to believe she could handle just about anything that came her way, but the past four days of being held captive by the outlaw gang left her doubting herself. Still tied to the outlaw leader, she lay curled up on her side under her blanket near the campfire. She'd heard the man talk about the plans he had for her, and she knew what fate awaited her when they reached the cantina. The thought of being forced to sell her body horrified her, and she'd been desperately trying to figure out a way to escape from the three killers. Mile after desolate mile of travel, riding double with Les Jackson had given her no chance to get away, though. She felt completely and utterly helpless, and that didn't sit well with her—not at all.

Dusty listened to the conversation now as the three men sat around the campfire, sharing a bottle of whiskey. Desperately, she wondered if there was any chance a posse could catch up with them and rescue her. She'd refused to give up hope for the first few days, but now, with each passing mile that took her farther and farther away from home, she was beginning to believe there was no one coming for her. She was on her own.

Drawing deep within herself, Dusty found the fortitude she needed.

She had to find a way to escape.

She could count on no one but herself.

Knowing the outlaws were drinking heavily tonight, she believed she might have a chance to sneak off if she could find a way to cut through the rope. Ever so carefully, she looked around and spotted a small rock within reach. She drew it to her and carefully began to rub the rope that bound her to Les Jackson against the rock's roughest edge. This bond would be the hardest one to remove, but it was the most important. If she couldn't free herself from it, she had no chance at all to escape.

A sense of renewed determination filled Dusty as she began to fight for her freedom. Time was running out. She had to do something fast.

Ugly Joe looked over at the outlaw leader, who was lounging across the campfire from him. "What do you think, Les? Ain't it time we found us some place to do some celebrating?"

They'd been riding hard since the holdup four days before, and he was more than ready to find a town with a saloon and some hot, willing women. He let his gaze rest on the girl curled up beside Les. She seemed to be asleep.

Les knew what kind of man Ugly Joe was, and he knew trouble would be coming if they didn't find somewhere to relax pretty soon. "I'm not sure we've outrun them yet."

"We know that sheriff from Canyon Springs is useless," Ugly Joe argued. "Even if he got up a posse, he'll never find us."

"No, he won't, but don't forget the Rangers. We took care of the one, but that don't mean there aren't others still after us."

Ugly Joe cursed under his breath at the thought of the Rangers. They were known to be relentless in their tracking. "Give me the damned whiskey."

Cale held out the bottle of liquor he'd been drinking and Ugly Joe snatched it from his hand.

"There ain't no reason to hog it all. There's plenty to go around," Cale told him.

"Not if I have my way," the other outlaw growled.

Les spoke up, recognizing Ugly Joe's bad mood. "Take it easy, boys. We'll ride for Flat Rock and stop there for a day or two just as soon as I'm sure nobody's on our trail. Then you can have yourselves some fun before I head down to the cantina to get my extra cash for the girl."

Cale didn't say another word. He knew how much Ugly Joe loved to fight, and the last thing he wanted to do was get into it with him over the liquor.

"Here, Cale. I got one bottle left," Les offered, pulling his own whiskey out of his saddlebag. "Ain't no reason we all can't share."

"I appreciate it," Ugly Joe said as he took the

bottle from Les and opened it to take a deep drink. "I owe you."

"I'll remember that."

They drank long into the night until the powerful liquor finally did its work and they all passed out.

The silence that overtook the campsite filled Dusty with hope. She'd never had much use for whiskey before, but she truly appreciated its numbing power over Jackson and his men as she carefully pushed her blanket aside and looked around. The three outlaws seemed to be sleeping soundly, and she knew this was her only chance to get away. It hadn't been easy freeing herself from the rope, but she'd done it. Now she just had to get as far away from the outlaws as she could before they woke up and realized she was missing.

Dusty silently arranged her blanket to make it look as if she were still curled up there sleeping. She thought about trying to get one of the guns, but the men were wearing their holsters and slept with their rifles right next to them. She would have no chance to grab one without being caught. She'd been lucky so far this night, but didn't want to push it. She would have liked to have taken one of the horses, but there was no way. Even as drunk as they were, the outlaws would awaken instantly if they heard the horses stirring.

Praying desperately that she could make her escape without waking them, Dusty crept into the darkness, determined to get as far from the campsite as she could before daybreak. She moved off in the direction they'd come, hoping the rugged terrain would help hide her trail. She hoped, too, that she might run into a posse from town. If she didn't—

Dusty didn't even let herself think about what could happen to her alone and on foot, unarmed and without food and water. She was going to do this. She was going to escape and find her way home, and then she was going to ride back with the law and help catch her father's killers. She had every intention of being there when the Jackson gang was brought to justice.

She'd heard Les talking about Texas Rangers being after them, too, but she'd seen no sign of anyone closing in. She hoped the Rangers were out there, but no matter what, somehow, some way, she was going to see the murderers pay for what they'd done. Her sadness turned to determination and fury as she fled into the night, and she knew that fury would sustain her.

Grant was up before dawn and saw the ominous red tint to the eastern sky as the sun rose. Knowing bad weather was coming, he was glad he hadn't bothered to wait for the sheriff and his posse. He hadn't seen any sign of them since he'd left town. If the posse had even found the trail, they were at least a good day's ride behind him, and he had no time to waste if he was going to catch up to Les Jackson.

Thoughts of Justine, or Dusty as Miss Gertrude had called her, haunted him as he rode out. She'd been so lovely, so feminine, the night of the dance, he found it hard to believe anyone would ever mistake her for a boy, even if she was wearing men's clothes. His expression darkened as he imagined what Les might have in store for her. He urged his horse on to a faster pace. Dusty was out there somewhere, and he wasn't going to quit until he found her.

Les woke up first and groaned. The liquor had worked its magic the night before, but now he was paying the price.

"Time to get moving," Les growled as Cale began to stir. His head was aching, and he was angry with himself for drinking so much. He knew it was going to be a long, painful day of riding. He sat up and looked over to where the girl was still curled up under her blanket. He figured with the noise they'd just made, she was faking being asleep, so he yanked on the rope that tied him to her, wanting to get her moving.

Les was shocked when the rope pulled free.

"What the—"

He ran over to her blanket and threw it back to find she was gone.

"What's wrong, Les?" Cale asked as he sat up quickly and looked over. One glance told him what he needed to know. "She's gone?"

Les was swearing vilely as he strode to where Ugly Joe was still sleeping. He kicked the other man angrily, demanding, "Where is she? What did you do with her?"

Ugly Joe was hungover and hurting. Getting booted in the side didn't sit well with him at all. He charged to his feet, ready for a fight. "What are you talking about?"

"I'm talking about the girl!"

"What about her?" In his fog from the drinking binge, he could only frown and stare stupidly at Les.

"Look, you dumb ass!" He pointed toward her empty bedroll.

Ugly Joe was as shocked as Les had been to find she was nowhere around. "I didn't do nothing with her. I passed out right after you did—" He liked a good fight, but he was in no condition to take on Les this morning, especially as mad as the outlaw leader was.

Les was still cursing as he began to look for her around the campsite. "She didn't get any of our guns and she didn't take a horse. She shouldn't be too hard to find."

Cale looked at him as if he were crazy. "You want to waste time looking for her? We gotta keep moving."

"I'm going after her," Les snarled as he went to saddle his horse.

Cale looked over at Ugly Joe, hoping he would try to help convince Les to change his mind, but the other man only shrugged. They had a better chance of avoiding trouble if they stayed together. There was safety in numbers. After all, they'd still seen no sign of Jim. There was no telling what had happened to their friend.

Cale and Ugly Joe went to saddle their horses, too. If they'd thought their previous days had been hard, today was going to be even worse.

Dusty was exhausted as daylight spread across the land. She hadn't stopped all night in her desperate flight, but now with the heat of the day coming, she knew she needed to find water and a place to hide out. The outlaws would be searching for her and she had to be careful not to give herself away. She kept looking for some sign of a posse, but could see no trace of anyone.

Dusty finally found a small spring and stopped long enough to drink her fill. She regretted deeply that she didn't have a canteen with her, but there had been no way she could have taken one without rousing the sleeping outlaws. Her thirst satisfied for the time being, she moved on, traveling another half mile before seeking cover deep under a rocky overhang. She was glad there were no snakes there, and took what comfort she could find on the hard ground.

"There's a storm coming," Cale pointed out, drawing a dirty look from Les.

"So ride harder," Les ordered.

Dark threatening clouds were gathering to the northwest, and he wanted to find the girl before the rain washed out her trail.

"We've been after her for more than two hours," Ugly Joe complained, "and we ain't found her yet."

"She's good at hiding her trail," Cale agreed.

"We keep riding much more in this direction, and we're going to find a posse from town, not the girl," Ugly Joe said.

Les was furious. He wasn't used to being outsmarted by anyone, let alone a female. He'd mainly wanted to find the girl to teach her a lesson for trying to escape from him, but this time he knew his boys were right. They had their money. It was time to take care of themselves and forget the runaway. Les figured she wouldn't last long on foot anyway with no food or water or weapon. Reining in, Les looked out over the rocky, rugged countryside but saw no trace of her.

"You're right, boys. It's time we headed for Flat Rock. I think there's some good times waiting for us there."

Ugly Joe and Cale shared a look of relief as they turned their horses and rode for Flat Rock. The wild town would be the perfect place to hide out and enjoy themselves.

Chapter Twelve

Grant dismounted to check the trail he'd been following. A crushed blade of grass assured him that he was heading in the right direction and that he was closing in on the outlaws. He looked out across the rugged terrain, but saw no sign of the gang anywhere in the distance. The best he could figure, they were still close to a good day's ride ahead of him. As determined as ever, he mounted up again and moved on, keeping an eye on the gathering clouds.

The deep rumble of thunder in the distance warned Grant that the threatening storm would break soon. Tracking on the rocky ground was hard enough as it was, but if the storm proved to be as severe as it looked, he knew it would wash out the trail completely. Best Grant could tell, Jackson and his men were riding southwest, so he would head that way once the weather cleared, and hope that he could find some sign of them again. They were not going to get away.

The wind picked up, and when lightning erupted from the clouds, Grant sought what shelter he could find beneath a rocky outcropping. He threw on his slicker and waited out the storm, frustrated by the delay but more determined than ever not to give up.

As he waited out the storm, Grant wondered where Frank was. He hoped his friend was hard on the gang's trail, too. He looked out into the downpour and prayed that Dusty hadn't been harmed.

Dusty stayed in her hiding place until long after the storm had moved through. The fierceness of it thrilled her even though she'd gotten wet. She didn't really mind the discomfort, because she knew that the heavy downpour had erased all traces of her passing. She waited until midafternoon before venturing out. When she saw no sign of Les and his men, she offered up a prayer of thanks as she moved on. Just because she couldn't see them right now didn't mean they weren't somewhere around, so she kept a careful watch as she started off in the direction of Canyon Springs again.

Hunger was her driving force and she began to search for anything that was edible. She found some persimmons and wild onions. They weren't much, but they offered some sustenance. She needed all the strength she could get to keep moving.

As the afternoon wore on, the heat grew unbearable, but Dusty didn't want to risk stopping to rest again. The danger was too great.

Thanks to the heavy rain, she was able to find a little more water than usual in this harsh land. At one small pool, she knelt down to cup her hands and get a drink. As she did, for the first time in days, she caught a glimpse of her own reflection. She stared at the image mirrored in the water, her dirty face and hair.

Had it only been a few days ago that she'd been "Justine"? When her hair had been done up with a feminine bow, and she'd worn a pretty dress and jewelry? It seemed an eternity since the night she'd felt like a princess out of a fairy-tale book, dancing with the stranger in town named Grant.

Grant—

She remembered how he'd appeared out of nowhere to save Francie from the drunken cowhands, and she wondered where he was now.

As soon as she had the thought, she grew angry with herself.

There was no handsome prince riding to her rescue.

Her father was dead.

She was alone, on her own.

She could count on no one but herself.

Tears blurred her vision, but she forced them away. This was no time to be weak. She could only think about staying alive.

She got up and kept moving.

It was dark when Dusty decided to take a chance and climb up a steep incline. She hoped to spot any campfires that were nearby, so she'd know how close the outlaws were to catching up with her. The footing was treacherous, but she made it, and her relief was great when she discovered no sign of any campfire back in the direction she'd come. She decided to check ahead of her, too, and it was then that she spotted a campfire's faint glow in the distance.

A torrent of emotions assailed her. She was torn between the joy of thinking it might be a posse from town, to the full terror of fearing it could be other strangers, as lawless and dangerous as the Jackson gang.

Dusty calmed herself and made her decision. She was getting weak and had been feeling a little dizzy. She'd found little water since earlier that afternoon, and needed a drink. She knew her best chance of survival was to make her way up close to the campsite and find out who was there. She was hoping to discover the campsite crowded with men from town. She was hoping to see the sheriff and her father's friends.

Though she was growing ever more unsteady, she made her way back down the incline and moved off toward the glow of the campfire more than a mile away.

Grant was glad the weather had cleared. He had been able to make up some of the time he'd lost by riding even harder that afternoon, but his mood was still troubled as he ate his sparse meal. Something was bothering him, and he wasn't quite sure what it was. The night seemed quiet enough. He'd seen no threat of any danger around, but he had a sense of uneasiness that left him more alert than usual. He went to check on his horse one last time, then sat back down by the fire, keeping his rifle close beside him.

Dusty moved silently through the darkness. She knew there might be a guard keeping watch, so she had to be careful. As she got closer to the light, she sought higher ground and tried to position herself so she could get a clear view of the campsite. In the distant glow of the small campfire, she could make out only one man. Lean and broad shouldered, he was sitting back away from the fire and was wearing his hat pulled down low, shadowing his face, so she couldn't make out his features.

Dusty's spirits sank when she realized it wasn't a posse from town. Fearful of being discovered, she started to move quickly away to find a place to hide for the rest of the night. Her sudden movements left her even more dizzy and disoriented. What little strength she had failed her, and she lost consciousness.

Grant had been getting ready to bed down when he heard the sound of someone moving in the underbrush. In a quick move, he threw dirt on the fire and grabbed his rifle as he dove for cover. He drew his sidearm and stayed down low, circling out away from the fading glow of the dying fire.

After several minutes' search, he spotted what appeared to be an unconscious man, lying facedown in the dirt, not too far off. He was cautious as he closed in. He'd learned the hard way that things weren't always what they seemed.

Grant thought he was ready for anything as he knelt beside the man and set his rifle aside.

He carefully turned him over, only to discover it wasn't a man at all.

It was Dusty—

Not Dusty the way he remembered her, but unmistakably the same girl—

And she was alive—

Everything Miss Gertrude had told him about the hardships in her life went through his thoughts as he stared down at her limp form. It was obvious she'd been through hell these past days.

Grant quickly holstered his gun and gathered her up in his arms. He could feel the heat of her body as he held her close, and he realized she was burning up with a fever. After grabbing his rifle, he carried her back to the campsite and laid her gently on his bedroll. He tried to make her comfortable on his blanket. He built the fire back up so he could see what he was doing, then checked her over for any injuries she might have suffered. He found her head wound right away and knew she was lucky to be alive. When he found no other injuries, he was relieved. He set to work cleaning up her wound and then soaked his handkerchief to wipe down her face and neck, hoping to cool her off and wash away some of the grime from her long days in captivity.

He found himself wondering how she'd managed to escape from the outlaws. She was proving herself to be an amazing woman, just as Miss Gertrude had claimed. He lifted his gaze to stare off into the darkness, wondering if the outlaws might be coming after her. If they were, it would give him the perfect opportunity to trap them, but he seriously doubted the killers would waste their time.

They had to know a posse from town was on their trail and that after escaping, Dusty would head back toward Canyon Springs. No, with the amount of money they'd stolen, it was logical for them to keep riding. They could buy themselves all the female companionship they needed at the next town they decided to stop in. They wouldn't risk their chance to make a clean getaway chasing after one girl.

Momentarily satisfied that there was no immediate danger, Grant concentrated on doctoring Dusty as best he could. He hoped she was strong enough to fight off the fever that gripped her. Throughout the long hours of the night, he stayed close by her side, watching over her.

"No, Papa! No!"

Her frantic cry jarred Grant awake in the hours just before dawn, and he quickly went to Dusty as she struggled to sit up in her delirium.

"Easy—" he said in a gentle voice as he took her in his arms, wanting to calm her terror.

"They shot him! They killed him!" she sobbed in her feverish, mindless torment. The confusion she was feeling showed in her eyes. She tried to focus, but the power of the fever left her disoriented and completely lost. She stared up at the man who was holding her. The dark shadow of several days' growth of beard along his hard, lean jaw gave him a dangerous look, and she suddenly fought against his hold on her. "Let me go!"

"Dusty, you're safe—"

"Where am I? Who—?"

"It's me—Grant. No one's going to hurt you," he assured her.

"Grant—" Dusty went still at his words. She believed she was only dreaming about her hero coming to save her. She felt certain that any second she was going to wake up and find herself a captive of the Jackson gang again. She closed her eyes against the misery of the thought.

"Dusty— Dusty girl, you're going to be all right. I've got you now."

The delirium of the fever overwhelmed her, and she faded into unconsciousness again.

Grant set to work once more, trying to cool her down, hoping the fever would ease up soon.

But it didn't.

Dawn found Grant still vigilantly at Dusty's side. As he watched the sunrise, he knew just how lucky she'd been to make it to his campsite. The thought of what might have happened to her if she'd lost consciousness all alone in the wilderness troubled him. Luckily, he'd been in the right place at the right time last night. He was thankful that he'd been there to help her, but he knew he was losing valuable time in tracking down the gang. There were no towns close by, so it was up to him to nurse her until she was strong enough to ride double with him. When she did get her strength back, he would take her to the nearest settlement and leave her there, where he knew she'd be safe, while he continued the hunt for Jackson and his men.

It was late in the day when Dusty began to stir. She opened her eyes to find the sun low in the western sky. Her thoughts were confused, and she frowned as she tried to figure out what had happened to her. The last thing she could remember was seeing a campfire in the distance and hoping it was the posse's campsite. She moved slightly, wanting to sit up, and realized she was lying on a blanket. Startled, she raised herself up on one elbow and fought off a wave of dizziness as she looked around. It was obvious the outlaws hadn't caught up with her for she wasn't restrained in any way, but there seemed to be no one around. She was alone. Bewildered, she managed to sit up as she tried to come to grips with all that had happened to her.

It was then she heard the familiar voice behind her.

"So you're finally stirring—"

Chapter Thirteen

Dusty gasped and looked around to find Grant Spencer walking back into the camp. She was stunned, and she was even more shocked to see that he was wearing a Texas Ranger badge.

"Grant—"

He saw her wide-eyed look of confusion and gave her a reassuring smile. "Yes, it's me."

"But Jackson and his men—" Fear gripped her as her horrible memories returned full force. She looked nervously around, ready to run if she had to.

"It's all right. You're with me. You're safe," he quickly assured her as he came to sit beside her.

She could only stare at him in confusion, trying to make sense of everything. "What are you doing here? How did you find me?"

"It was more that you found me. I was camped out here last night when I heard a noise in the darkness and went to check. I found you unconscious, burning up with fever."

"I had a fever?" That made sense to her, considering how confused she felt.

"A bad one." He touched her forehead carefully. He was relieved to find the fever had finally broken. "Yes, you're much cooler now."

His gentle touch sent a shiver of sensual awareness through Dusty, surprising her. She looked up into his eyes. She knew now he had truly saved her life. "Thank you."

Grant saw the depth of her innocence, and a surge of protectiveness filled him. It was a powerful emotion unlike anything he'd ever experienced before. No matter what, he had to keep her safe. "I'm just glad I was here." He wondered what the odds had been of her escaping the gang, covering all those miles on foot and then finding her way to his campsite.

"So am I." Her words were heartfelt. She looked down at his badge. "You're a Ranger—"

"Yes. I'm after Jackson and his men."

"Jackson—" Horror trembled through her. Her eyes filled with tears as she looked up at Grant, her expression bleak. "I want them caught— I want them to pay for what they've done."

"Don't worry. I'm going to get them," he assured her.

"Where's the posse? Why aren't you riding with them?"

"I heard the sheriff was getting one up, but I didn't have time to wait for them to get organized. I knew Jackson would be moving fast and I wanted to be on his trail as quick as I could."

"Good." She heard the determination in Grant's

voice and knew he wouldn't quit until he'd caught the outlaws. He was, after all, a Texas Ranger. They were the best.

"Why did they decide to take you with them after the robbery?" he asked.

Dusty looked saddened for a moment and shuddered at the memory of the outlaw's hands upon her. "They were searching us for valuables, and discovered I was a girl. From what little I heard them say, Jackson was planning on selling me to a whorehouse south of the border."

Grant had suspected that was Jackson's motive, but the confirmation still enraged him. "Did they hurt you in any way?"

"No," she replied quickly. "Jackson wouldn't let the other men touch me. He said the people at the whorehouse would pay more for me if I was a virgin—" The very thought sickened her.

Grant reached out and drew her to him, wanting to comfort her. She rested her head on his shoulder as he held her protectively in his arms.

He knew just how lucky she was to have escaped when she did. "How did you manage to get away?"

"They started doing some heavy drinking the other night and luckily they all passed out. They had tied me up, but I'd been working on the rope all night with a sharp-edged rock and managed to get free without Jackson realizing it. I was scared to take off on foot, but I didn't have any other choice. I knew if I tried to steal a horse, they would probably wake up, and I had to get out of there."

"You're every bit as smart as Miss Gertrude said you were."

"You spoke with Miss Gertrude?" she asked in surprise, drawing away to look up at him.

He nodded to her. "She was the one who told me about the robbery and that you'd been taken. I had no idea you rode shotgun for your father on the stage."

Anguish and guilt overwhelmed her. "But what good was I? Riding shotgun, I was supposed to keep everyone safe, but I couldn't save my father or Matt— They're both dead because of me—"

"Stop, right now," he commanded, fully understanding what she was feeling, but wanting to ease her pain and feelings of guilt. "Jackson and his men had the ambush all planned out. They knew exactly what they were doing. You took a head shot. You're lucky to still be alive, outgunned the way you were."

"I don't think so." In her heart, Dusty felt as if a part of her had already died. Only her driving hatred for Jackson and his men gave her the inner strength she needed to keep going. "My father should never have been killed! He and Matt were good men. They'd never hurt anybody. Those outlaws murdered them both—and for what? Money? Jackson and his men think money is more important than people's lives?"

"There are bad people in this world. That's why I became a Ranger. I want to stop as many of them as I can, and I'm going to stop Jackson and his men— real soon."

"And I'm going to help you," she said fiercely.

"No, you're not," he stated. "You've got to get your strength back so you can travel, and then I'm going to take you to the nearest town and set you up there until you can catch a stage for home."

She glared at him as she told him, "But I heard Jackson and his men talking, and I know where they're going."

"Where?"

She was defiant as she met his challenging gaze. "I won't tell you—not unless you agree to take me along."

"No. You're not riding with me." He knew the danger involved.

"Look, Ranger, I can do this," she argued, getting furious. "Besides, you need me. It's not like you've been having any luck finding Jackson and his gang before now."

Grant's anger and frustration grew at her words.

She went on. "Don't you think it would be a lot easier knowing where they're heading than just trying to find their trail and track them after all this time? And especially after the bad storm the other day?"

"Bringing them in will be dangerous. They're killers."

"I know, and I learned all about danger riding shotgun with my father," she came back at him.

"All right," he said, aggravated, but knowing he had no choice except to play along with her. "Where did they go?"

Dusty stared at him in a bit of surprise. He'd

given in so quickly that she was immediately suspicious. Grant wasn't the kind of man who gave up easily or backed down. She wondered what he might be planning. She'd heard Jackson and his men say they were riding for Flat Rock, but she wasn't going to trust Grant completely with that information, not just yet, not until they were well on their way after the gang. Instead, for right now, she told him, "They said they were riding to Gold Canyon." Gold Canyon was on the way to Flat Rock. She would tell him the full truth as they got closer.

Grant nodded. "All right, we'll head out at first light."

"I'll be ready."

"You better eat and drink something. I don't want you slowing me down."

"I won't slow you down."

"Remember that."

"Don't worry. I can keep up with you. All I need is my own horse, a gun and a change of clothes, and I'll be ready to go after Jackson and his men." The thought of bringing in her father's killers strengthened her spirits.

Grant had learned over the years when to pick a fight, and he knew this wasn't the time. He fully intended to leave her in the nearest town, just as he'd originally planned. He would leave money behind for her and ride out while she was sleeping. She'd have no choice but to go on home.

"When we get to town, I want you to see a doctor and have him take a look at your wound. I don't want to chance your coming down with a fever again while we're on the trail."

"All right." She knew he was right as she reached up and gingerly touched the wound where he'd bandaged it. She remembered how she'd thought he was a guardian angel the night of the dance. He had shown up at just the right moment to save Francie, and now he'd appeared out of nowhere when she'd needed him most.

He got his canteen and gave it to her. "Drink up while I fix you something to eat."

"Thanks. I think I am a little hungry," she admitted. The outlaws had barely fed her, so it had been days since she'd had anything substantial to eat.

Grant prepared the food he had with him, and he was glad to see that Dusty scraped her plate clean. That was a good sign.

"We'll leave early," he told her later as he got ready to bed down across the campfire from her.

"I'll be ready whenever you are," she promised. "Are you sure you don't want your blanket?"

"You keep it. I'll get another one when we reach town."

Dusty thought about offering to share it with him, but then realized that wouldn't be proper. Not that there was anything proper or ladylike about her current situation. She was quiet for a minute as she watched Grant try to get comfortable on the hard ground. She would forever be thankful he was the one she'd run into out here in the middle of nowhere.

"Grant—" She said his name softly.

Grant turned and looked over at her. "What? Is something wrong?"

"No— No, I just wanted to tell you how grateful I am for everything you've done for me. You're a very special man, Grant Spencer. I probably would have died if you hadn't saved me— Thank you."

"You're welcome. Now, get some sleep. We've got a lot of miles to cover tomorrow."

"Good night," she said, and she closed her eyes, feeling safe and protected for the first time in days.

Grant watched her for a moment longer and then settled back to try to get some sleep himself. He was so tired, he didn't think the hard ground was going to bother him at all tonight, and he was right.

The horror of the gunshots came out of nowhere. She tried to help, but the bullet grazed her and she fell. The next thing she knew, they were dragging her away and she saw her father, lying dead near the stage—

Dusty came awake with a start, her heart pounding in agony as the memories of that day haunted her dreams. She didn't even try to fight back the tears that threatened as she gave vent to the deep, abiding, heartrending misery that filled her soul.

Her father was lost to her forever—

It had been terrible enough when she'd lost her mother so suddenly, but now, to lose her father, too—

She buried her face in the blanket to muffle the

sound of her crying. She tried to tell herself that she had to be strong, but right then, nothing mattered except the sorrow that overwhelmed her.

Grant awoke suddenly and was instantly aware that something was wrong. He didn't make any fast moves, but looked around, trying to figure out what had disturbed him. It was then that he heard the sound of Dusty crying, and he immediately got up and went to her.

"Dusty—"

At the deep, reassuring sound of Grant's voice so close beside her, she looked up to find him there.

He saw the pain in her expression and took her in his arms. Her vulnerability touched him deeply, and he wanted to ease her sorrow. She went willingly into his embrace and clung to him as she continued to weep. When, at last, her crying quieted, he looked down at her.

"Dusty—" he said softly.

In the soft glow of the moonlight, their gazes met. The harshness that was their reality vanished. Time stood still as he slowly bent to her and claimed her lips in a gentle kiss.

At the touch of his lips on hers, Dusty was lost. She surrendered to his embrace, lifting her arms to link them around his neck. Grant stretched out beside her, bringing her fully against him as he deepened the kiss.

Dusty had never imagined a man's embrace could be so exciting. She clung to Grant, needing his nearness, needing his strength, loving the feeling of being so close to him.

Grant was caught up in the thrill of her kiss. He had known from the night of the dance that she was beautiful and desirable, and it was wonderful to have her in his arms at last. He wanted her as he'd never wanted another woman. They shared kiss after heated kiss, and then his lips left hers to trail a path of excitement down her neck.

Dusty gasped at the sensations his lips were arousing in her as he pressed heated kisses to her throat. In her innocence, she arched instinctively against him, an unknown need growing deep within her.

"Oh, Grant—" she whispered.

He lifted his head to gaze down at her. "You are so beautiful—"

His words sent a shiver of delight through her, and she drew him back down to her, kissing him hungrily. When he slipped his hand inside her shirt to caress her, she gasped at the intimacy. She had never known a man's touch before. With utmost care he kissed her again, a passionate, possessive exchange.

Grant wanted her. There was no doubt about that, and total innocent that she was, he knew she was his for the taking. It was that revelation that helped him hang on to the last shred of his iron-willed self-control.

It wasn't easy for Grant, but he ended the kiss and leaned back, drawing her head down to rest on his shoulder as he kept his arms protectively around her. What he really needed to do was to put some physical distance between them, but he knew she needed comforting, and he wanted to reassure her that she was going to be all right and that she was safe with him.

Dusty felt strangely abandoned when he ended the kiss. She had been lost in the wonder of his embrace and the glory of his kisses. She couldn't imagine why he'd stopped. She raised herself up on her elbow to look down at him, her expression troubled. "Grant— What's the matter? Why did you stop kissing me? Did I do something wrong?"

Her complete innocence touched him deeply. "Hardly," he assured her, smiling tenderly at her. He saw the confusion in her eyes and told her, "You were doing everything right. That's why I had to stop."

Dusty suddenly understood, and she lowered her gaze and looked away, embarrassed.

"It's all right." He kissed her one last time and then nestled her back against him. "You need to rest. Tomorrow's going to be a rough day."

She nodded, but didn't speak.

Grant was all too aware of her nearness as she curled against his side and closed her eyes. He struggled for control and knew he was going to have to find a way to deal with having her so near—especially when they started riding double together in the morning. It wasn't going to be easy.

Even as weary as he was, Grant knew he wasn't going to get much sleep tonight, not with Dusty so close. He shut his eyes and tried to think about tracking Jackson and his men. He wondered, again, where Frank was and if he was closing in on them, too.

He was surprised to find a few moments later that Dusty had fallen asleep.

Chapter Fourteen

Grant had known he wouldn't get much sleep holding Dusty in his arms, and he'd been right. He looked down at her now as she lay so close beside him, sleeping peacefully, and was struck again by what a beautiful woman she was. She appeared delicate as she rested, but he knew how strong she truly was to have survived all she'd been through.

As Grant thought about the days to come, he grew worried. He was glad she'd shared the information she'd had about the outlaws' plans, but he had to find a way to leave her somewhere safe so he could track down the killers. She'd suffered enough already. He didn't want to put her at any more risk. He knew she would be furious with him, but he hoped she would forgive him when he brought the gang in.

The night aged, and Grant managed to move away from Dusty without awakening her. He got up to start quietly breaking camp so they could ride out at dawn. They had a lot of miles to cover, and he couldn't afford to lose any more time.

* * *

It was still dark when Dusty awoke. She was surprised to find that Grant was already up. She didn't say anything for a moment, taking the time to watch him as he moved about the campsite. Her gaze went over him, taking in his broad shoulders and lean waist. In the light of the low-burning fire, she could see the dark shadow of several days' growth of beard. It added an element of danger to his look, but she knew he was no danger to her.

Far from it.

The memory of his kiss and touch brought a sensual smile to her lips as she continued to watch him, and she knew in that moment she was falling in love with him. The realization surprised her even as it seemed so simple. From the first moment she'd seen him at the dance, she'd known he was a very special man.

"Good morning," she said in a sleep husky voice.

Grant quickly looked her way and smiled. "You're awake—"

Her heartbeat quickened at his smile. "I can't believe I slept so well."

"I'm glad you did. It'll help you get your strength back. How do you feel this morning?"

"Much better."

"Good."

"How soon do you want to head out?"

"As soon as it's light. It's a long ride to the next town. We've got a lot of miles to make up."

"I know. I'm sorry I slowed you down," she said as she sat up and got ready to help him.

"I'm just glad you found your way here."

"So am I. If it hadn't been for you—"

Grant went to her and took her in his arms. "Let's don't even think about that."

She looked up at him and couldn't help herself. She asked, "What should we think about?"

He hadn't meant to touch her this morning—it was going to be difficult enough riding with her. He'd been trying to distract himself, thinking about the job he had ahead of him, but having her in his arms was a temptation he couldn't resist. He kissed her, a hungry, devouring kiss that left them both breathless. He was glad he had enough willpower to put her from him when he finally broke it off.

Grant gave her a wry smile. "We have to think about getting some breakfast and saddling up."

He said no more, but set about doing just that. They ate what little food he had brought with him and then got ready to ride.

Grant had been wondering which would be safer for her—putting Dusty in front of him so he could keep his arms around her, or positioning her behind him. She seemed to have most of her strength back, so he decided to leave the decision up to her.

"I'll ride behind you," Dusty said, after he'd asked her. "That way, if we do run into any trouble, I won't be in your way."

"That's fine," he agreed.

Grant mounted first and then took her arm to pull her up behind him. He'd been relieved that she would not be sitting before him. That was until she wrapped her arms around his waist to hold on. The feel of her pressed so intimately against him left him gritting his teeth as they started out. His only solace was that she would have been an even bigger temptation, riding in front.

Sheriff Perkins faced the men in his posse as they got ready for another day of hard riding, trying to find the Jackson gang. "Boys, I hate to say this, but I think it's time we give it up and head back to town."

Most of the men murmured their agreement, but Rick and Fred confronted him angrily.

"We can't give up!" Rick argued.

Fred added, "Rick's right. We can't quit tracking the gang. Not after what Jackson and his men did! These men are cold-blooded murderers!"

The sheriff didn't like anyone contradicting his orders, especially not Fred and some young smart-ass banker man. "You think I don't know that? I know damned well what kind of men Les Jackson and his gang are, but that storm ruined any chance we had of staying on their trail. They've done got away from us, and there ain't nothing more we can do."

"You're wrong. We can keep circling out and try to pick up their trail again. We know they're out there somewhere—with Dusty!" Rick wasn't a very good tracker, but several of the men riding with them were.

Fred looked to two older men, Ralph and Al, who were the best trackers. "Rick's right. You're not going to just give up, are you?"

Ralph and Al shared a frustrated look before answering.

"I ain't one to quit if I think there's a good chance of picking up the trail again, but we haven't seen any sign of them for days now," Ralph said.

"I know what you're feeling, Fred. I want to catch them killers, too, but we're wasting our time," Al agreed. "We're riding in circles going nowhere. Jackson and his men are long gone."

"But what about Dusty?" Rick argued.

Fred glared at them. "Dusty's a good girl, and now she's out there somewhere with them—"

"I know what you're saying, but they're gone. We're not going to find them," Ralph told him.

"So we just quit?"

"We ain't got much choice," Al said in disgust. Charley Martin had been a good friend of his, and Matt had been his friend, too. Knowing what plans they probably had for Charley's daughter sickened him, but there was little more they could do. Sure, they could keep searching, but after all this time, the chances were slim to none that they'd find any clue to the direction the gang had ridden.

Rick and Fred knew they were helpless to save Dusty on their own, and the realization left them even angrier. They stalked away from the other men.

"I don't know what I'm going to tell Francie and my wife," Fred said, disgusted and sickened by the way the manhunt had turned out.

"I just wish there was something more we could

do." Rick was miserable over their failure. He
thought of Francie and knew how heartbroken she
was going to be when they returned to town without having rescued her friend.

"So do I, Rick. So do I," Fred sympathized.

Their moods were dark as they mounted up and
got ready to head back to Canyon Springs empty-
handed.

Sarah was hard at work cleaning out one of the
stalls in the stable when she looked up to find the
Ranger standing silhouetted in the doorway. Tall
and broad shouldered, he was a commanding presence as he stood there watching her for a moment.

"Are you sure you should be up and moving
around this much?" she asked, surprised to find him
there. She'd known he was getting stronger, but this
was the first time he'd ventured so far from the
house on his own.

"I'm feeling much better thanks to your doctoring," Frank told her with an easy grin.

"Some of the ranch hands have had broken ribs
before, and it's taken them a good couple of weeks
to be able to get up and around again."

He chuckled. "But I'm not on your payroll."

She couldn't help laughing, too. "If you're this
eager to work, maybe I should hire you on."

"I just may take you up on that. I think you'd be
a pretty good boss lady."

"There aren't a lot of men who think like you do.
Most of them won't take orders from a woman."

"Depends on the woman," he answered. "I saw

your father and brother ride out earlier with some of the men. Are they coming back anytime soon?"

"No. They're out checking stock. I don't expect them until close to suppertime. Why?"

"Well, since I'm moving now, I wanted to ride up to the place where you found me. I thought if I took a look around, I might find something that would jar my memory."

"Are you sure you're up to riding?"

"Yes," he answered without hesitation, growing serious, "and I can't go on this way much longer. I have to find out who I am and why someone wanted me dead."

Sarah had known this moment would come eventually. "All right," she said, moving out of the stall. "Let me clean up a bit and we'll take a ride over there."

She made short order of washing up at the pump and then quickly saddled the horses for them. She could tell it frustrated the Ranger not to be able to help her, but she refused his offer, not wanting him to strain himself just yet. They'd see how he felt later after making the ride. She swung up on her horse and watched as he mounted, too. It took an effort for him, she could tell, but he seemed comfortable enough once he was in the saddle.

"Ready?"

"Oh, yeah," he answered, his expression serious as they started out.

Sarah kept their pace steady, yet slow as they covered the miles to the site of the ambush.

"Do you want to ride up on the trail or go down where Andy and I found you?"

"Both," Frank answered. He didn't know if this would help jar his memory, but he knew it was worth a try. As his physical wounds healed, it was harder for him to deal with his memory loss, and he was beginning to find that he didn't seem to be a very patient man.

They started up the narrow trail on the steep hillside, and Sarah reined in about halfway up. Frank reined in beside her and studied the craggy, rocky hills that surrounded them. An eerie feeling came over him, but he could remember nothing about the day of the ambush.

"From what Andy and I could figure out, you were probably right about here when they shot you. There's no telling where they were hiding. There are any number of places up there where they could have gotten a clear shot at you. Your horse must have thrown you, because we found you down at the bottom of the ravine."

Frank dismounted and walked over to the edge to stare down at the rocks below. "You never saw any sign of my horse?"

"No. Nothing."

He looked around a little more on foot, hoping to find his saddlebags or anything he might have dropped that would give him a clue to his past, but found nothing. He mounted again and looked over at Sarah.

"Let's take a look at the place where you found me."

Again, she led the way, taking him back down the trail and then around to the narrow passageway that ran through the bottom of the ravine.

"You were lying just about here," Sarah told him as she stopped and got down to help him search for anything he might have lost during the fall.

Frank joined her, looking up to study the steep hill, trying to summon a memory of exactly what had happened that fateful day, but there was nothing. He looked around the area carefully, but, again, found nothing.

"I'd hoped this would help, but I don't remember a thing." An anger was growing inside of him that he knew he had to control.

"It will. You'll remember. It's just going to take a while longer," she said sympathetically.

"But how much longer?" He walked slightly away, not wanting her to see how tortured he was by not knowing.

Sarah could feel his pain, and she went to stand beside him, putting a hand on his arm to reassure him. "I wish I knew the answer for you, but I don't."

Frank looked down at her, seeing all her kindness and generosity—and her beauty. "You're one special woman, Sarah."

Sarah's breath caught in her throat as he slowly took her in his arms and drew her to him. His lips sought hers, tentatively at first. When she met him in that exchange, he deepened the kiss, pulling her even closer.

For a moment, Sarah was stunned, and then the reality of being in his embrace overwhelmed her.

Her Ranger had survived. He was healing, and he was kissing her.

Her heartbeat quickened as she wrapped her arms around him and returned his kiss in full measure. She had known him for only a short time, but she knew in that moment, even without finding out the truth of his past, that she loved him. He might not have his memory, but he did have the inner strength and fortitude it took to get through these hard times. She had no doubt in her mind or in her heart that he was a good and honorable man.

When, at last, the kiss ended, they drew slightly apart to stare at each other with a sense of wonder.

"Thank you, Sarah," he said solemnly, lifting one hand to tenderly caress her cheek. "If it hadn't been for you and Andy coming to help me that day, I wouldn't be standing here right now."

She smiled up at him. "I am just glad that we were here—"

"So am I."

Frank kissed her again, loving the feeling of having her so close to him. He felt a sense of loss when they finally moved apart.

"We'd better head back—" she said, knowing it would be best if they returned to the ranch before her father did. There was no telling what kind of trouble her father might cause if he found out she'd been riding alone with Grant, even though it was broad daylight.

They mounted up and started back out of the ravine.

"I'm sorry riding up here didn't help you remember anything," Sarah said as she looked over at him.

"It was worth a try. I was hoping to find my saddlebags or something else that might help me figure out who I really am and where I was going."

She couldn't help herself as she fought to keep from smiling. "You did remember something—"

He frowned as he glanced over at her. He had no idea what she was talking about.

"You remembered how to kiss—" She put her heels to her horse's sides and rode on ahead of him.

Frank couldn't help himself. He started grinning and quickened his pace to catch up with her.

Chapter Fifteen

Dusty hung on tightly to Grant as they covered the long miles toward Bluff Mesa. It was a rough ride in the stifling heat, but they finally caught sight of the town at midafternoon.

"We're almost there," Grant told Dusty.

"Doesn't look like much of a town," she remarked.

"It's not, but the last time I rode through they did have a doc." He didn't mention that there was also a stage that came through a couple times a week. His plan was to make sure she could get back home on the stage, while he rode on after Jackson. It wasn't going to be easy to get away from her, but he would do it. He had to. There was no way he could concentrate on doing his job when she was so close. Why, just riding now with her holding on to him so tight was a constant reminder of the temptation she was to him. He knew she would be furious with him when she discovered what he'd done, but he would make it up to her by bringing her father's killers to justice. "How's your head feeling after all this riding?"

"It's hurting, but nothing like what it was. I'll be all right."

"I don't want to take any chances with you. We'll see if we can find the doc first thing."

Dusty didn't say a word. She just kept her arms wrapped around him as they rode the final distance into Bluff Mesa.

"And I'm going to call you 'the kid,'" he told her. "It'll be easier that way to keep up your disguise."

She had wondered what they were going to do. She wondered, too, if they would be sharing a room at the hotel. She wasn't sure what his plan was, but she was certain he'd already thought it all through.

The townspeople who were out on the sidewalk stopped what they were doing to watch them pass by.

Grant reined in out in front of the hotel and helped Dusty down before dismounting himself. He led the way into the hotel, leaving her to follow him up to the desk.

"Afternoon, Ranger," the clerk said, spotting his badge right away. "What can I do for you?"

"I need two rooms. One for me and one for the kid," he said.

"For just one night?"

"That's right. We're just passing through."

Dusty was surprised Grant was getting her a room of her own, but she was also grateful for it. It was one thing sleeping at a campsite together. It would be another to share the more intimate space of a hotel room—and since she desperately wanted to take a bath, it would prove awkward.

The clerk pushed the registration book toward Grant and waited while he signed them in. He eyed the youth standing behind the Ranger and could tell the kid had been through some hard times lately.

"Well, Ranger Spencer," the clerk said, taking the time to read their names, "that'll be a dollar."

Grant paid the clerk. "I was wondering, is there still a doc in town?"

"Sure is. Dr. Benton is just one street over, about a block down."

"Thanks."

"Anything else?"

"Yeah, I'm going to need a bath when we get back, and I think the kid could use one, too. Take care of that for us, will you?"

"I sure will," the clerk promised, handing him two keys. "Just stop here when you come back from the doc's and I'll get your baths going."

Grant got his gear and rifle from the horse and went up the narrow stairs with Dusty to check out their rooms. They were located next to each other at the far end of the hall and faced the front of the building. Though they were sparsely furnished with only a single bed and washstand in each one, after the last few nights on the trail, they looked like luxury to Grant.

"I'll take this one," he said, putting his gear in the room closest to the stairs. He had a plan, and he was going to make it work. He had to get to Gold Canyon as fast as he could—without Dusty.

Dusty didn't say anything. She went into the

room next to his and sat down for a moment on the welcoming comfort of the bed. "I think I'm going to sleep like a baby tonight."

"I know what you mean," he agreed, as he came to stand in her doorway. "Let's go find that doc, and when we're finished with him, we'll stop by the general store to get supplies and see about finding you some clothes."

Dusty self-consciously glanced down at her dirty boys' clothing. "I'd appreciate it."

They left the hotel together and made their way to the doctor's office. They were glad to find there were no other patients waiting when they went in.

The tall, silver-haired physician greeted them cordially as they entered. He saw the bandage on the youth's head and asked, "What happened to you, young man?"

It hadn't occurred to Dusty until that moment that the doctor might need to examine her closely, and she suddenly worried that he would discover she was a girl. She looked at Grant and knew she had to tell the truth.

"It's a long story, Dr. Benton," she began.

"You might as well tell him everything," Grant said, then turned to the doctor. "But we'd appreciate it if you'd keep what we tell you to yourself, Doc."

"Of course, Ranger—?"

"Spencer, I'm Grant Spencer, and this is Dusty Martin."

"Actually, Dr. Benton, my name is Justine," Dusty confessed.

The doctor gave her a surprised look. "I see."

Dusty quickly told him the whole story of the robbery, her kidnapping and how she'd managed to get away and find Grant's campsite.

The doctor was impressed as he looked at her. "You are a very strong woman, Justine."

"I'm my father's daughter," she said sadly.

The doctor patted her hand. "I'm sure he'd be very proud of you right now." When she didn't say anything in response, he directed, "Come on back here to my examination room and let me take a look at your wound."

Dusty and Grant went into the other room with the doctor. He helped Dusty to sit on the examining table and carefully removed the bandage.

Grant stood back and was silent while the doctor checked her over. He could see the pained look on Dusty's face as the physician cleansed the wound.

"You came very close to being killed, Justine," Dr. Benton told her honestly. He looked up at Grant. "You did a good job patching her up. There doesn't appear to be any infection. I have some salve that will help the wound heal, and I can give you some laudanum to ease the pain."

He set about applying medication to the wound and after rebandaging it, he gave Dusty the laudanum.

"Will you be in town long?" he asked.

"No, we'll be leaving tomorrow," Grant answered.

"Well, good luck to you both, and Ranger Spencer—"

Grant looked at him questioningly.

"I hope you find that gang real soon."

"So do I," he replied seriously.

Grant paid the physician and they started from his office.

"Do you want to go on back to your room or go get supplies with me?" he asked Dusty, noticing that she looked a little pale.

"If you don't mind, I think I need to go to my room and rest for a while."

Grant returned to the hotel with her and ordered her bath before leaving to take care of the rest of his business. His mood was serious as he bought the supplies he would need and picked out some new boys' clothes for her.

"How often does the stage come through town?" Grant inquired of the store clerk.

"There will be one through tomorrow afternoon."

"Thanks."

The timing would work out well. He would leave Dusty enough money to pay for her ticket and expenses going home, and he would be long gone before she had any idea what he was up to.

Grant took his horse down to the stable before returning to the hotel to order his own bath. When he asked about getting something to eat, the clerk told him there was a restaurant down the street and Grant decided he and Dusty would go there once he'd gotten cleaned up. As he started to enter his room, he thought about checking on Dusty to give her the new clothes he'd bought her. It sounded very quiet in her room, though, so he figured that she was probably resting and he decided not to bother her right then.

When his bath was brought up to his room, he stripped down and climbed into the tub of hot water. It had been quite a while since he'd had the opportunity to take a real bath, and he set about scrubbing himself clean.

It was as he was washing up that his gaze fell on the clothes he'd bought for Dusty. Though he didn't want to admit it to himself, he knew he was going to hate leaving her. He tried to tell himself that he wouldn't miss her company any more than he missed Frank's, but Grant knew that wasn't true. He'd never known anyone like her before in his life, and under other circumstances, he knew things could have been very different between them.

Grant was worried about how Dusty was going to react when she discovered what he'd done the following morning. He hoped she'd be smart enough to understand why he was leaving her behind. He grimaced at the thought of how angry she was going to be, but knew it had to be done this way.

He was riding to Gold Canyon alone.

He wanted her safely back home where she belonged.

He would check on her after he'd finished with the outlaw gang, but he didn't want her along on the chase.

Grant was real glad he wasn't going to be there the following morning when she got up and found the note he was going to leave her.

* * *

Dusty had been thrilled over the chance to bathe. She'd washed quickly and then realized to her disgust that she would have to put her filthy clothes back on until Grant brought her new clothes. Instead, she just wrapped herself in the sheet off the bed and stretched out to wait for his return. She hadn't meant to fall asleep, but she had.

Dusty came awake suddenly and stared around the hotel room in confusion for a moment until she remembered where she was. She heard someone in the room next door and knew Grant was back. Eager to get her clean clothes, she threw on the old, dirty ones and hurried over to his room to see what he'd brought her.

"Grant, I heard you moving around and knew you were back—" she was saying as she knocked once, then opened the door and walked into his room.

The sight that greeted her left her speechless for a moment, for there was Grant, sitting in the bathtub right in front of her.

"Oh—my—I didn't realize—"

Dusty blushed at the sight of his broad, hard-muscled chest, and she quickly looked away as he grabbed the towel he had near at hand and used it to shield his lower body from her view.

"I'll be done here in a few minutes," he told her.

Was that laughter in his voice?

"Well, I—um— The clothes—" She still didn't look back in his direction.

"On the bed," he directed.

Grant waited as she got the things he'd bought for her and quickly started for the door.

"Thanks," she muttered, keeping her gaze averted.

"Get changed," he said. "We'll go get some dinner as soon as I'm through here."

He watched her leave the room and close the door firmly behind her. He finished his bath and wrung out the soaked towel, grinning wryly as he thought of how lucky it was that he'd kept it so close by. By the time he got dressed and shaved, he was ready for a hot meal.

Dusty quickly stripped off her filthy clothes and threw them aside, eager to don the new things he'd bought for her. She glanced in the small mirror over the wash stand and saw that it was still Dusty staring back at her, not the feminine-looking Justine she'd been at the dance. Grant had bought her new work pants and a blue shirt rather than a dress

A vision of how she'd looked in the pretty gown the night of the dance came to her, and she winced, thinking that night when she'd been "Justine" had been a lifetime ago. She sighed and turned away, knowing it had been nothing more than a fantasy.

It wasn't much longer before she heard Grant's knock at her door, and she quickly answered it. She was surprised to find him freshly shaved and dressed up in clean clothes. She had become so used to seeing him with a rugged growth of beard that she was again struck by what a truly handsome man he was.

"Are you ready?" Grant asked, his gaze going over her new pants and shirt.

"Yes, and thanks again for the clothes. I'll pay you back when we get home."

"There's no need. I'm glad to help. Are you hungry?"

"Starving."

"Let's go take care of that. I think we could both use a decent meal."

"I know we could."

They left the hotel and went to eat at a small restaurant nearby. The food was delicious, and they ate a hearty dinner of steak, potatoes and greens, along with hot, fresh bread, and apple pie for dessert.

"I take it you liked the cooking here," Dusty said, smiling at Grant as he finished off the last of his pie.

"It's been a long time since I had a meal this good."

"I know. Me, too. My mother was a real good cook, but after she died and I started riding with my father, we never had much time for fixing up big meals." As always, thinking of her father hurt. She was beginning to wonder, too, what she was going to do with her life after the Jackson gang was brought to justice. "What about you? Did you enjoy meals with your family?"

"My mother died when I was nine. My father was sheriff of the town we lived in, so he wasn't around a lot."

"I understand. With Pa driving the stage, we didn't get to see much of him either."

Grant paid for their dinner and they started back to the hotel.

"How are you feeling?" he asked.

"My head is still a little sore, but other than that I feel all right."

"You might want to take some of that medicine the doctor gave you so you can get a good night's sleep." Grant was hoping that a dose of the potent painkiller would have Dusty sleeping soundly all night.

"You're right. It's been a while since I've slept the night through."

Grant glanced down at her as she walked by his side in the fading daylight. He remembered the first time he'd seen her at the dance and all that had happened to them since that fateful night that brought them together.

They reached the hotel and went upstairs, then stood together for a moment in the hall outside their rooms.

"Do you need anything else tonight?" Grant asked, concerned about her. He knew he wouldn't see her again for a while, and, oddly enough, he was beginning to wish he could take her with him. Life was never dull when she was around—why, he couldn't even take a bath in peace.

Dusty couldn't tell him the true answer to that question. She wanted to be with him tonight, sleeping in his arms as she had been the night before beside the campfire. Only when he'd been holding her so close, kissing her, had she forgotten all the ugliness that had come into her life. "I think I'm all right."

"Don't forget your medicine."

His thoughtfulness touched her, and if they hadn't been standing right there in the middle of the hall, she would have drawn him down to her for a kiss. "I won't. Good night. I'll see you in the morning."

"Good night." Grant avoided saying he'd see her in the morning. He stood there, watching as she started into her room.

Dusty was ready to close the door, but in that instant, she knew she couldn't. "Grant—there *is* something I need—"

Chapter Sixteen

Grant was puzzled by her answer and followed her into her room. It wasn't often he was caught off guard, but Dusty always managed to surprise him. When he stepped inside, she pushed the door shut and walked into his arms, kissing him. He was stunned, but only momentarily. His own desire took over, and he gathered her close, deepening the kiss as he crushed her to him.

"Oh, Grant—you don't know how thankful I am that you found me—" she whispered as she clung to him.

"And *you* don't know how thankful *I* am," he told her, bending to her to kiss her again.

Grant hadn't meant for this to happen. He'd tried to banish the memory of having her in his arms, but her kiss destroyed any hope he'd had of ignoring the feelings she stirred in him. He'd never felt this way about a woman before, and as she moved sensuously against him, he enjoyed the thrill of having her near. Sweeping her up into his arms, he moved to the bed with her and they stretched out together on the welcoming softness, glorying in the ecstasy of being together.

Dusty was innocent to the ways of loving. Yet she gave herself over to him, responding fully and without reserve as his mouth moved hungrily over hers, creating a burning fire of desire deep within her. She began to move restlessly against him, unaware of what her sensuous movements were doing to Grant. She just knew that she needed him.

Grant held her close, thrilling to the passion she aroused in him. She was unlike any woman he'd ever known, and he knew deep in the heart of him that he had to make her his own. Without interrupting their kiss, he unbuttoned her shirt and parted it, pushing down the binding she wore to disguise the fullness of her breasts.

Dusty gasped at the intimacy of his caress, and when he shifted lower to press heated kisses against her bared flesh, she had never known such bliss. She arched to him, in love's age-old offering.

Grant was caught up in the pure pleasure of being so close to her. Her wanton response to his kiss and touch was arousing him as nothing else could.

He needed her.

He wanted her desperately.

He had to make her his.

But his last shred of sanity told him this was wrong, and somehow, he found the inner fortitude to rein in the power of his desire for her.

He could not make love to her and then ride off and leave her there all alone.

There was nothing he wanted more than to love her and make her fully his, but Grant knew this wasn't the time or the place.

Agony tore at him as he softened the hunger of his kisses and carefully drew her blouse closed over the pale beauty of her bared breasts.

Dusty had been lost in the magic of Grant's loving, but this time when he pulled away, she understood she'd done nothing wrong. The feelings she had for him grew, for she realized how much he respected her not to take what she had so freely offered. She stayed in his arms, her eyes closed, cherishing the hard strength of his body so near to her.

Grant was struggling as he lay back with his eyes closed and his jaw locked. Logic had returned with a vengeance, and it was warring with his desire. He could not use Dusty this way. He respected her too much. He vowed then and there that he would come back for her as soon as he was finished with Jackson.

She would be his.

It was just a matter of time.

Determined to hang on to that thought, he moved away from her side and stood up.

"It's best if I leave you now." He gazed down at her, visually caressing her flushed cheeks and slender form.

Dusty was caught up in the power of her need for him. She wanted to launch herself into his arms and drag him back down on the bed with her, but she saw the steely look in his eyes and held herself back. She said nothing.

Grant went to let himself out, then paused to add, "Don't forget to take your medicine."

With that, he left her, closing the door silently behind him.

Dusty stared at the closed hotel room door, and then got up to take the laudanum so she'd be well rested enough to keep up with him in the morning.

Grant returned to his room. He packed up his personal belongings and then wrote a note to Dusty. He planned to slip it under her door along with the money she'd need to make the trip back home. After packing up his gear, he waited close to an hour, just to make sure she would be sound asleep when he left his room.

Grant was very careful when he finally ventured out. He moved in total silence to her door, slipped the note and money underneath it, and then left the hotel. The clerk wasn't at the front desk, and he was glad. He didn't want anyone to know what time he'd ridden out of town.

The less Dusty knew, the better it would be for the both of them.

A short time later, Grant rode away from Bluff Mesa and disappeared into the night.

Dusty slept soundly. She awoke feeling quite refreshed, surprised to find it was broad daylight already. She worried for a moment about Grant, wondering where he might be, then realized he'd probably deliberately let her sleep late. She appreciated his thoughtfulness, and excitement filled her at the thought of seeing him that morning. She was eager to get dressed and go find him so she could kiss him again. The thought that they were going to be together from now on lifted her spirits. She knew this morning that she loved him, and she couldn't wait to tell him.

Dusty quickly sat up on the side of the bed, her back to the door, and took a minute to organize her thoughts. The medicine had done a fine job. She felt rested and her head wasn't nearly as sore as it had been. Grant had been right about going to see the doctor. She got up and started to move around the room. She made short order of washing up, then started to gather her few belongings. As she bent to pull on her pants, she spotted the folded piece of paper on the floor near the door.

She was puzzled and went to pick it up, wondering who could have left her a note. She was greatly surprised when she unfolded it and found the money inside. Then she looked at the bottom of the note and saw Grant's signature. She suddenly grew worried and quickly began to read what he'd written.

> *Dusty,*
>
> *I had to stay on the trail of the Jackson gang. I've left you enough money to pay for your ticket home. There's a stage passing through this afternoon.*
>
> *I'll come and find you in Canyon Springs after I bring the gang in. Be careful and take care of yourself.*
>
> *Grant*

Dusty stared down at the note he'd left her in complete and utter disbelief. Her heart was broken.

Only moments before, she'd believed herself to be falling in love with Grant.

She'd thought he was a good man.

She'd thought he was a man of his word.

But now she knew the truth.

She'd meant nothing to him.

Once he'd gotten the information about the gang's whereabouts from her, he had ridden off and left her behind.

Pain shattered Dusty, and tears blurred her vision. She was torn between heartbreak and anger. After one anguished sob, anger won out. Fury motivated her as she hurried to get dressed and grab her belongings. She stopped to count the amount of cash he'd left her, and smiled grimly, knowing it should be enough to take care of what she needed today.

Dusty stopped at the front desk to speak to the clerk. "Did you see Mr. Spencer leave this morning?"

"No. I haven't seen him at all."

"Thanks."

She left the hotel knowing then that he'd ridden out of town during the night. He had a big head start on her, but one thing he didn't have—he didn't have the real information about where the gang was going.

Angry though she was about the situation she found herself in, Dusty mentally patted herself on the back for not trusting Grant completely. Oh, he'd been nice to her, and he'd taken care of her, and he'd certainly wooed her enough to make her let her guard down, but now she knew the truth about him.

And now, he was going to learn the truth about her.

For the first time since reading his note, she managed a tight smile. She couldn't wait to see the expression on Grant's face when she caught up with him in Gold Canyon. She was going to enjoy that moment a lot.

Dusty went to the stable and worked out a deal with the stable owner to get the horse she needed for the trip. She had enough cash left to buy some supplies and to purchase herself a gun. At least Grant had been generous with the money he'd left her. She went to the restaurant and ate a big breakfast, knowing it would be the only decent meal she'd have for some time to come, and then she mounted up and headed for Gold Canyon.

The ride wasn't going to be an easy one, but nothing was going to stop her from going after Les Jackson and his men.

Nothing.

It had been a long, hard trek to Gold Canyon, but Grant reached the outskirts of town late the following morning. He'd stopped only for a few hours just before dawn to get a little sleep and then had started out again, determined to find the killers.

Grant hadn't been through Gold Canyon very

often. Mostly, it was known as a quiet town. He'd been a bit surprised when Dusty had said the outlaw gang planned to go here, but then, knowing Jackson and his men, they probably figured nobody would be looking for them in a peaceful little place like this. Grant knew he had to be ready for anything and everything.

Grant spotted the sheriff's office up ahead and decided to stop there first and talk to the local lawman.

Sheriff Becker was sitting behind his desk and looked up as the tall stranger came through his office door. There was an air of danger about the man, the way he walked, the way he wore his gun, and then the lawman saw his Texas Ranger badge. He stood up to welcome the newcomer.

"I'm Tom Becker. The sheriff of Gold Canyon."

Grant came forward, introducing himself. "I'm Ranger Grant Spencer."

"Well, Ranger, what brings you to our town?" the sheriff asked as he came around the desk to shake hands.

"You been having any trouble in town lately? Any strangers doing some wild drinking?"

Sheriff Becker frowned, surprised. "No. Things have been nice and quiet lately. We've all been enjoying it. Why?"

"I'm on the trail of Les Jackson and his gang, and I had reliable information that they were heading here."

The local lawman looked troubled. "I haven't seen or heard anything, but if I do, I'll let you know."

"I appreciate it. I'll be taking a look around and probably staying on for a day or two."

"If I can help you—"

"I'll let you know."

The sheriff could tell the man didn't expect to need any help. "Wasn't it the Jackson gang that robbed the stage from Canyon Springs?"

"Yes. They killed the driver and the man riding shotgun."

"They're a mean bunch."

"I know, but I'm going to put an end to their killing ways."

"Good luck to you, Ranger Spencer."

"Thanks."

"Hotel's just one block over."

Grant nodded and left the office. He didn't have time to make small talk. He had a job to do.

Dusty had said the gang was supposed to be in town, but he had a strange feeling that something just wasn't right. He took a very careful look around as he rode over to the hotel and rented a room for the night. After settling in, he made his way to the saloon to see what he could learn there.

Chapter Seventeen

It hadn't been easy making the ride to Gold Canyon all alone, but then Dusty knew her life was not going to be easy now. She was on her own, and she'd just proven to herself again that she could do whatever she set her mind to.

It had been hard getting to town before nightfall, but Dusty knew the worst part was yet to come. Soon, very soon, she was going to have to face down Grant. She was a little worried that he might have ridden on already, but she hoped he would still be in Gold Canyon, lying in wait for the gang to show up.

She smiled grimly.

If he was waiting for Les Jackson and his men to ride in, she was going to have a surprise for him.

She was the one who was going to be riding in— not the Jackson gang.

Her anger had sustained her across the seemingly endless miles, and she was thankful now for that anger. It gave her the strength she needed to keep going and to do what she had to do.

Gold Canyon seemed quiet as she rode down the main street. She wanted to leave her horse at the stable and get a room at the hotel without anyone noticing her. Things went well. It didn't take long to stable her horse and then, carrying her gear, she made her way to the only hotel in town. She was glad the man tending the stable had told her there was only the one hotel. If Grant was in town, he'd be spending the night there.

Inwardly, she smiled.

She was tempted to take a look around town, but she didn't want to risk running into Grant on the street. She planned to check out the hotel first and see if she could discover what room he was staying in. She couldn't wait to see the look on his face when she confronted him.

Grant thought he was so smart. Well, she'd show him. His kisses had only been meant to distract her from what he was really planning. She recalled the way he'd reminded her to take her medicine. She was certain now, he'd told her to take it so she wouldn't hear him leave the hotel during the night.

Dusty was careful as she entered the small hotel. It was late, but there was still an older, balding man at the desk.

"Need a room, sonny?"

"Yes, sir," she replied respectfully.

"You all by yourself?"

"I am."

"Let's see your money." He eyed the youth skeptically, wondering if the kid had the cash to pay.

"How much you charging?"

"You wanting a bath?"

"No."

"Then fifty cents will do it."

Dusty handed him the money, and he pushed the registration book across the desk and went into the small back room to get the key to the room.

Dusty quickly scanned the names of the few other people staying in the hotel that night and was grimly rewarded when she saw that Grant had signed in. According to the book, he was staying in the room number six. She made up a fake name and signed herself in, then shoved the book back across the counter.

"Here you go," the clerk said, coming out to hand over the key. "You're in room ten. It's up the stairs and about halfway down the hall on the right."

"Thanks."

The clerk went back to his duties.

Dusty was glad that he paid no more attention to her as she went up the narrow staircase to the second floor. The hallway was narrow and the only light came from a single lamp on a table at the far end of the hall. Even so, she could make out the numbers on the doors and she was glad to find that her room and Grant's were only one room apart on the back side of the building. She didn't see any light coming from under his doorway and figured he was down at the saloon or checking things out around town. Either way, it gave her the time she needed to plan exactly what she was going to do.

Deciding to be completely daring, since there was no one else around, Dusty stopped and very carefully tried to open the door to Grant's room. As she'd expected, it was locked.

All the same, she was determined to be waiting for him when he showed up later that night. If she'd had a hairpin with her, she knew she would have been able to pick the lock and let herself in, but "the kid" didn't have any need for hairpins. When she'd bought her supplies in the last town, they hadn't been on her list of necessities. The thought left her half smiling as she went into her own room, locking the door behind her.

After lighting the lamp on the small dresser, Dusty left her things on the bed and took a quick look around. She parted the curtains to find her window had been left partially open and that it looked out over the alleyway. To her delight, she discovered that there was a small covered porch on the back of the building.

Dusty opened her window farther and leaned out to look around. She was glad to find that she could climb out the window onto the porch roof and make her way over to Grant's room—if she was careful. She'd have to be quiet since she'd have to pass another room on the way. She just hoped whoever was staying there wouldn't see her. She hoped, too, that Grant had left his window open. There was no light coming from his room, so she couldn't tell just by looking. It was going to be tricky enough getting there, but if she found out the window was shut and locked, she was going to have some real trouble getting in.

The dark window told her he wasn't there yet, though, and that was good.

She wanted the element of surprise on her side tonight.

He'd surprised her by leaving her behind.

Now it was her turn to get the upper hand.

Dusty turned back into her own room and took the time to quickly clean up. With the day's grime washed off, she was ready. After turning down the lamp, she climbed out the window.

It was a clear night and the moon was close to full, so she could see fairly well. Ever so carefully, she made her way along, staying close to the building and taking care not to look down. It was a steep drop to the alley, and she didn't even want to think about what might happen if she fell. Her relief was great when she made it past the first hotel room without being seen. Painstakingly, she inched the final distance to the window to Grant's room. She was excited—and relieved—to find the window was partially open as hers had been.

Dusty pushed it all the way up so she could climb inside and then quickly looked around the room. There was enough moonlight for her to see Grant's things on the bed, so she knew she was in the right place.

Now, it was just a matter of time.

Soon, very soon, Grant would be back, and she'd be ready for him.

She sat down in the straight-backed chair next to the washstand on the far side of the bed to await his arrival.

* * *

Grant finished off his whiskey and looked around the quiet saloon. He'd taken his badge off for the evening, wanting to keep his identity quiet for a while.

"You want some more?" Victor, the barkeep, asked, coming up to him with the whiskey bottle in hand.

"No, I'm done for the night," Grant told him.

"So how soon you riding on?" Victor had tried to get the stranger talking, but he hadn't had much success.

"I'll be here another day or two," Grant answered.

"Well, come on back in. I'll always have whiskey for you, and my girls would be more than glad to entertain you—if you need some entertaining," Victor said, nodding toward the two saloon girls who were moving around the room, flirting with the men at the tables.

Grant glanced over at the saloon girls in their low-cut, revealing dresses and smiled. "I'll keep that in mind."

He left the saloon then, knowing the only woman he wanted to "entertain" him was somewhere on a stage heading for Canyon Springs. He gave a weary shake of his head as he stopped on the sidewalk to look up the street. All was quiet and peaceful, and, again, he had the feeling that something wasn't quite right, but he couldn't figure out what was troubling him. He always trusted his instincts, though, so he was extra careful on his way back to the hotel.

The small lobby was deserted, and he went on

up to his room, ready to get some much-needed rest. It had been a long two days, and he needed to sleep He hadn't slept in a real bed for quite a while now. He reached the door to his room in the dimly lighted hall and had just started to walk in when he saw it—

The window was fully open and he'd left it up only a few inches earlier that day—

His survival instincts took over.

He might not have found the Jackson gang, but it looked like the gang had found him.

Grant went for his gun as he dove into the room. He expected a blaze of gunfire to erupt as he made his move. He rolled to his knees and came up ready for trouble, only to find himself staring at Dusty, sitting on the chair in his room in the dark, watching him.

"You—!" he snarled, almost shaking with relief that he hadn't opened fire on her. In disgust, he slammed his sidearm back in the holster as he got to his feet.

"You were expecting someone else?" she asked sarcastically. "Or, maybe, you weren't expecting me at all—?"

"Dusty—" Grant's tension turned to anger as he stormed over to the dresser and struck a match to light the lamp there. He turned it up all the way and then stalked back to shut the door. Only then did he turn to look at her again.

"I take it you're surprised to see me," she taunted.

"You're supposed to be on a stage going home," he declared.

"I decided that wasn't what I wanted to do. I have some unfinished business to take care of. I have to find Les Jackson."

"I don't want you riding with me, woman," Grant argued.

"You don't have a choice, Ranger man," Dusty said smugly, giving him an arrogant look.

"Oh, yes, I do," he countered.

She gave a low, sarcastic laugh. "You think you do, but I know better."

"What are you talking about?" He suddenly wondered what she was up to.

"Back when I first told you that I knew where Jackson was going, I got a little suspicious when you agreed to take me along so quickly. I decided not to tell you everything I knew. You see, you're not about to find Jackson and his men here in Gold Canyon."

"What do you mean?"

"I mean, they were never coming here—"

He swore under his breath at her revelation. "You mean, I wasted all this time riding here for nothing?"

She just smiled coolly at him as she stood up and crossed the room to face him. "No, Ranger, you didn't waste any time. That's why I rode out after you as soon as I got up this morning. I told you they were heading here to Gold Canyon because—"

"You lied to me—" he challenged. He stared down at her, his gaze hard.

Dusty didn't care how angry he was. "No. I didn't lie to you. I just didn't tell you everything."

"So there's more to this— Where are they?" he demanded.

She was enjoying paying him back for what he'd done to her. She answered, "We'll need to pack up and head out real early in the morning—but, of course, riding out early is normal for you, isn't it?"

It wasn't often Grant found himself at a disadvantage. It annoyed him greatly that Dusty had managed to trap him this way and force him to her will. He told himself it didn't matter. He told himself the only thing that mattered was bringing in the murderous gang, but it didn't ease his irritation at her wiles.

Grant realized resentfully that he'd met his match in this woman.

Grant also realized his instincts had been right about Gold Canyon. The gang wasn't in town and never had been. It truly was the peaceful, quiet place that it seemed.

It was hard for him to do, but he swallowed his pride and answered, "You're right. I do like to get an early start. I'll expect you to be ready."

Dusty walked to the door to let herself out. "I'll be waiting for you, Ranger."

Grant stood there staring at the closed door with a rueful look on his face.

Chapter Eighteen

Francie was in the kitchen helping her mother when she heard a loud knock at the front door.

"I'll get it," she told her mother, quickly wiping her hands on a towel before going to answer the door. She opened the door to find one of the young boys from town there.

"Miss Francie! Miss Gertrude sent me down here to get you!" Tommy said.

"Why? What is it?"

"The posse just rode in!" With that the youth turned and ran off.

"Mother!" Francie shouted.

Marlene heard her daughter's frantic cry and rushed out to the front hall. "Who was it? What's wrong?"

"Tommy just came to tell us the posse's back!"

They shared a worried look.

"Did he say anything else?"

"No—"

"Let's get down to the jail," her mother said, her mood guarded. "Give me a minute to finish up what I was doing in the kitchen."

It didn't take Marlene long to rejoin Francie, and they hurried from the house to the sheriff's office.

They soon found out that word had traveled fast. There were a lot of the townsfolk gathering there. Marlene and Francie could see most of the men who'd ridden in the posse standing there with the sheriff, but they didn't see Fred or Rick, and wondered where they were.

"All right, all right, folks—" Sheriff Perkins called out, trying to calm the crowd. He only wanted to say this once and get it over with.

"What happened?" someone asked.

"Did you get 'em?"

Miss Gertrude elbowed her way to the front of the crowd to challenge the lawman. Her expression was fierce as she looked up at him and demanded, "Where is she? Where's Dusty?"

The sheriff ignored her for the moment as he moved to stand on the boardwalk in front of his office. "Here's what happened, folks. We tracked them for days, but lost their trail after a fierce storm washed through."

"You mean they got away from you?" Miss Gertrude accused, voicing the outrage of the whole town.

Sheriff Perkins knew he had to face up to the truth and admit the posse's pursuit had been a failure. "Yes. They got away from us."

Marlene was furious. "Where's my husband? Where's Rick?"

"Down at the stable," Perkins snarled, and with that he turned and went into his office, slamming the door shut to block out the yelling of the angry people. The crowd slowly began to move away in disgust.

Francie burst into tears as she fell into her mother's arms. "Oh, Mama— Where is she?"

Marlene held her close, trying to think of something to say, but she could think of nothing to cheer her. Privately, she wondered if they would ever see Dusty again.

Fred and Rick had stabled their horses and were coming back up the street as the sheriff stormed off. They hurried to the women.

"Francie—" Rick had seen her break down and start crying, and he wanted to comfort her somehow.

Francie lifted her head to find the handsome young banker standing there with her father, the two of them looking like defeated men. "Oh, Papa— Rick—"

"Fred?" Marlene said his name tentatively, wanting to hear his version of what had really happened on the trail.

"We wanted to keep searching for them, but Sheriff Perkins gave it up," Fred said, feeling like a total failure as he faced the women's despair.

Francie left her mother's embrace and went to Rick, touching his arm supportively. "What can we do now?" she asked, desperate.

At that moment, Miss Gertrude joined them. She'd heard Francie's question and spoke up. "We do the only thing we can do—we wait for our Ranger to show up. Grant will bring Dusty back."

They looked in surprise at the iron-willed old woman.

Miss Gertrude went on. "I knew Sheriff Perkins was useless from the start. I told Grant as much when he was getting ready to leave. If anyone can find Dusty, he will. You'll see."

"Do you really think he can find her, when the town's posse couldn't?" Marlene asked.

Miss Gertrude lifted her chin, her expression proud as she responded, "Grant Spencer is a Texas Ranger. He'll find Dusty and he'll bring her home. He's no quitter like Perkins."

Francie thought of Grant and how he had helped her and Rick the night of the dance. Her spirits lifted.

"You're right, Miss Gertrude. He won't give up." Rick was still angry over the sheriff's decision. "I should have ridden out with Grant."

"Well, don't you go feeling bad," the older woman told him. "You're a good man, Rick. You did what you thought was right."

"I just wish we could have rescued her."

"We all do," Francie said quietly.

Rick looked at Francie and then at her mother. "Would it be all right if I paid your daughter a visit later today, Mrs. Randolph?"

"Why don't you join us for dinner tonight?" she invited.

"I'd be honored," he accepted quickly.

"What about you, Miss Gertrude?" Francie asked. "Would you like to have dinner with us tonight? We'll be eating around six."

"Thank you. I'll be there," she said.

Rick left them to go home and get cleaned up.

Marlene glanced from her daughter to her husband. "This is so sad."

"Poor Dusty—" Francie said, her voice filled with a world of sorrow and pain.

When they met up to ride out of Gold Canyon the following morning, the tension between Grant and Dusty was real. They eyed each other skeptically, and neither of them spoke unless it was absolutely necessary.

Grant was furious because she still hadn't told him where they were heading, and it was obvious she had no intention of telling him anytime soon. He'd kept pace with her, trying to figure out which towns lay along the route they were traveling and wondering how long it was going to take them to get there.

The first night out, they made camp just before dark.

Dusty knew the time was coming when they were going to be facing down Les Jackson and his men—probably the very next day—and since she didn't have her shotgun with her, she wanted to get in some practice shooting her handgun. She set up some rocks on a ledge a distance from the campsite and practiced drawing and shooting. She was decent, but she wasn't as good as she wanted to be. She just hoped that if she did have to take a shot at one of the outlaws, she could at least wing them.

Grant was watching her from where he was sitting by the fire. He could tell she was no novice. She knew what she was doing, but he also knew she could use a little help. He got up and went to stand beside her.

Dusty had been very aware of him watching her every move. She'd tried to ignore him and had managed pretty well until he came over to her. She glared up at him. "What?"

"You want some advice?"

"Sure," Dusty said, sliding her gun back in her holster.

"You're used to using a shotgun, right?"

"Yes, that was what I always carried when I was working with Pa."

He nodded. "I can tell you know how to shoot—just try to make your draw smooth and in one motion. Try it again."

Dusty did, but her aim was still off.

"Here, let me help you."

Grant moved behind her and positioned her correctly.

Dusty wasn't quite sure how to react at having him so close to her. Mad as she was at him, she didn't want to be reminded of the power of his kiss or touch.

Grant, too, was well aware of Dusty's nearness, but he wanted to focus on teaching her the best way to improve her aim. He knew it could mean the difference between living and dying when they faced down the outlaws. He worked with her for a few minutes, helping her correct her aim, then moved away to watch her practice some more.

Dusty resented the fact that she'd had to take direction from Grant, but she also appreciated his taking the time to help her.

"Thanks. That does make a difference," she said as she holstered her gun, and set about cooking some beans and bacon for them.

"Good."

They ate dinner and then bedded down on opposite sides of the campfire.

"Good night, Dusty."

"Good night, Grant."

Neither was willing to say any more.

With the dawn, they were up and on their way again.

By noon, Grant finally figured out their destination.

"So they rode to Flat Rock," he stated flatly, looking over at her.

"And with any luck at all, they'll still be there when we show up. How do you want to handle this?" she asked, more than ready to follow his lead now. "What do you want me to do?"

He gave her a cold sidelong glance as he continued to ride. "So now you're willing to listen to me?"

She returned his icy regard without showing any signs of backing down. "I'm going to do this—with or without you."

Her words and defiance annoyed him.

She went on, her determination showing in her fierce expression. "We can do this together, Grant, or we can part company right now. You know where the gang is, just like I do. It's up to you whether we ride in together or not, but one way or another, I'm going to see Les Jackson and his killers brought in."

Grant reined in and looked at her seriously as she halted beside him. In that moment, he knew he had just taken on a new partner. "Well, partner, the first thing we're going to do is slow down. I don't want to ride into Flat Rock in broad daylight. It'll be easier to do what we have to do after dark."

Dusty had to admit, she was taken aback by the change in him. "Are you serious?"

His dark-eyed gaze challenged hers. "I've never been more serious. Just don't be afraid to use your gun if the need arises."

"I won't," she promised.

"All right, let's see if we can find some shade and rest up for a while. This might turn out to be a real long night."

Grant spotted a mesquite tree not too far off and rode there. They dismounted and went to sit beneath it.

"How much do you know about Flat Rock?" Dusty asked.

"It's pretty much a lawless town. I'm sure that's why Les picked it. He probably figured that since there was no sheriff to deal with, he and his gang would be safe to hide out there for as long as they wanted to."

"We're going to prove them wrong," Dusty said fiercely.

"And we might even get some help—"

She frowned at him. "How? If there's no law in town, who's going to help us?"

"Frank Thomas. He's the other Ranger I was riding with. We split up to follow the gang when they separated, and I haven't heard from him since. I know he's out there on Jackson's trail somewhere." Grant looked out over the countryside, wondering again how his friend was doing.

"Maybe when we ride into Flat Rock, we'll find out he's already arrested them," Dusty offered, allowing herself to smile slightly at the thought.

"Frank's certainly capable of it, and that would be some real good news," Grant agreed. "We'll be finding out soon enough."

Chapter Nineteen

Once Frank had started feeling better, he'd moved out to stay in the bunkhouse with the hands. He would have his full strength back soon, and he knew it was time he took some action to figure out the truth of who he was. He'd hoped the ride to the scene of the shooting would stir his memory, but it hadn't worked out that way.

The only thing stirred up was his desire when he kissed Sarah. But he couldn't let himself think about any kind of relationship with her until he knew his past.

He might have a wife and children—a family waiting for him to come home.

He had no idea.

His mind was still a blank.

Frank had come to recognize a few things about himself, though. He definitely was a man of action. He instinctively knew it wasn't normal for him to just be sitting around waiting for things to happen. He was looking forward to the day when he was healthy enough to go hunting for the truth of his past.

There was one other thing he'd discovered about himself. Staying in the bunkhouse with the ranch hands, he'd learned he was a pretty good card player. The hands got a poker game up some evenings, and he'd proven himself to be sharp. Frank had joked with the men that if he never got his memory back, he could become a gambler and just move from town to town, earning his keep playing poker in the saloons. Though the thought had made him smile at the time, he'd known it was something he'd never do. Living that kind of life held no appeal for him. There was more to him than that.

It was almost dark when he saw Sarah riding back in, so he went over to the stable to talk to her. She'd been out working stock that day, so he hadn't seen much of her. He found her tending to her horse as he came to stand in the stable doorway.

"Been working hard?" he asked.

She had been worrying about her father as she'd ridden back up to the ranch house, but just hearing her Ranger's voice eased her mood. She smiled as she turned to greet him, realizing she thought of him as *her* Ranger now. "Harder than you," she teased.

"That's not difficult to do these days," Frank countered

"How are you feeling?"

"Better. I think in another week, I should be about back to normal—whatever 'normal' is."

"We can always use another hand here on the ranch," she told him.

"I appreciate the offer. You were looking worried when you rode in. Did you run into some trouble today?"

"No, I was just thinking about my pa—"

"You knew he was going into town today, didn't you?"

"Yeah, and that's why I was worried. There usually is trouble if he stays in town too long. He starts drinking and his mood can get ugly." She turned away, not wanting to say more about her father's abusive ways.

"Sarah—" Frank moved to put a hand on her shoulder and turn her back around to face him. "You know if you ever need anything—I'm here." His dark-eyed gaze met and held hers.

Sarah felt her heart actually skip a beat at the look of concern she saw in his eyes. Except for Andy, who was so much younger than she was, she had never really had a man in her life who cared for her and wanted to protect her. "Thank you."

"No," he said in a low, soft voice, "thank you—"

The temptation was there, and he had no desire whatsoever to resist it. Ever so slowly, he took her by the shoulders and drew her to him for a kiss.

Sarah didn't even consider resisting. She had done nothing but think about the kiss he'd given her the other day, and she willingly met him in that embrace, returning his kiss full measure.

Frank was stunned for a moment by her response, and then he just relaxed and enjoyed it. He knew he shouldn't be kissing Sarah, but right then, he didn't care. He needed the feel of her in his arms, willing. Had he not been aware that some of the other hands were around, Frank might have swept her up and carried her to one of the piles of clean straw in the stable, where they could enjoy themselves. Instead, he just savored this stolen moment of closeness.

"I did need that," Sarah said when they finally ended the kiss and put some distance between themselves.

"Like I told you," he said, grinning at her, "if you ever need anything, I'm your man."

Sarah liked that thought. "I'll remember what you said," she assured him, returning his grin.

Luckily, they were a respectable distance apart when Andy came into the stable, looking for her.

"Sarah, Pa's still not back," he told her.

"That's what I was afraid of," Sarah said in disgust. "Maybe he'll spend the night in town and sleep it off."

"It'd be better that way," Andy remarked.

Frank could hear the uncertainty and terror in the boy's voice and felt a stirring of understanding and sympathy. He put a hand on Andy's shoulder.

"I was just telling your sister, if you ever need any help, you just let me know."

Andy was surprised by the edge of fierceness in his voice. "You'd help us?"

"Of course. You helped me. We have to take care of each other. That's what friends are for."

"I got dinner going, Sarah," Andy said, then turned to look at Frank with almost heroic adoration in his expression. "Do you want to eat with us up at the house instead of with the hands, Ranger man?"

"Why, I'd like that a lot, Andy. Thanks for asking."

"Let's go. It's almost ready."

"You two, go ahead. I'll finish up here and be right with you. I hope you made something good tonight. I'm real hungry," Sarah said, and she watched them walk from the stable together. She felt a warm glow within her at the sight of them. The Ranger was exactly the kind of man Andy needed in his life—a man who was strong and honest and kind.

She hurried to finish her chores and then followed the men up to the house. She went straight to her room to wash up before joining them in the kitchen for the meal.

Andy had made stew and there were some leftover biscuits from breakfast to go with it. The stew smelled delicious.

"I'm glad I taught you how to cook," Sarah said as she sat down at the table.

Andy said grace, and they all dug in, enjoying the meal and the time together.

But even though Andy and Sarah did have a good time, they were ever aware that their father could ride in at any minute. They had to be ready for whatever might happen when he did.

"You've never mentioned your mother," Frank said, thinking that she'd died. "Has she been gone long?"

Andy looked quickly at his sister, while Sarah tried to keep her expression from revealing too much.

"She's been gone for about five years," she answered.

Frank realized how young Andy had been when he'd lost his mother. "That was a rough time for you."

"Yeah," Andy began, wanting to tell Frank everything, "we woke up one morning and she was gone."

Frank thought he meant she'd died of a fever or something sudden overnight. "Was it a bad fever?"

They both looked up at him quickly.

"No, you don't understand," Sarah began carefully. "Our mother left us. She ran off, and we haven't heard a thing from her since."

"Pa was so mad—" Andy had been young, but he still remembered all the heartbreak that morning when he'd gotten up and tried to find his missing mother.

Frank was shocked by the news. "I'm so sorry."

"So are we. We still miss her, but—" Sarah let it drop. "We're doing all right. Pa's kept the ranch going and we've got each other, so things are good."

Andy looked at her, then added a little sullenly, "Most of the time."

"All right, let's enjoy what's left of our dinner," Sarah said, changing the topic. "It's almost time to start cleaning up the dishes."

"I'll be glad to help out," Frank offered.

"Good!" Andy was happy for the offer for he hated doing women's work. Cooking a meal was one thing, but dishes and actual housework were another.

It was an hour later when Frank bid them good night. He gazed at Sarah longingly for a moment before leaving the house. He was almost aching with the need to have her back in his arms, but with Andy so close, there was no privacy. He wanted to respect her and honor her, so he put the thought from him as he made his way back to the bunkhouse.

A few of the men already had a poker game going, and Frank joined in. He'd already won enough to pay back the money they'd loaned him the first time he'd played with them, so they were all eager for the chance to get back what he was regularly winning from them now. He knew, too, playing poker would take his mind off Sarah, and right then he needed to be distracted.

Sarah gave Andy a hug as they started to get ready for bed.

"Do you think Pa is going to show up tonight?" Andy was nervous at the prospect of their father riding in drunk.

"If he does, you just stay in your bedroom. I'll take care of him."

"Are you sure?"

"I'm sure." She gave him another reassuring hug, then kissed him on top of his head. "Now, go on and get some sleep."

"You, too."

"And don't forget to say your prayers, young man—"

"I won't," he promised as he disappeared into his room.

Sarah undressed and put on her gown. As she settled into bed, she found herself unable to sleep.

Her Ranger was in her thoughts, and she couldn't stop thinking about how wonderful it had been to kiss him in the stable. Even as she relived the thrill of his embrace, a sense of sadness overtook her. She wanted him to stay with her forever, but she knew that wasn't going to happen. It probably wouldn't be too much longer before he got his memory back. Once he did, she was sure that he was going to leave.

Sarah forced the thought away, and closed her eyes. She was determined to enjoy what time they had together. The future she would deal with when it happened. There was no point in worrying about it now for there was absolutely nothing she could do to change what would happen.

A tear traced a path down her cheek as she tried not to think about the day when her Ranger would ride away.

Chapter Twenty

Les, Ugly Joe and Cale had been in Flat Rock for a few days, and they'd been having such a good time that they'd given no thought to moving on. They were winning when they gambled, and they were making the saloon girls at the Hitching Post Saloon earn their keep. Life was good for them—real good.

It was after dark, and Les and Ugly Joe were in a high-stakes poker game when Cale decided to go down to the stable to check on their horses. He'd been drinking in the Hitching Post since mid-afternoon and felt the need to get outside.

Melody had heard him say where he was going and tried to stop him from leaving. She stood seductively in front of the swinging doors to tempt him to stay and go upstairs with her.

"You sure you want to leave so soon, Cale?" she purred.

"I'll be back in a while," he said. "Wait for me."

"But what if I want you—now—" Melody gave him her most alluring look as she reached out to put a caressing hand on his chest.

Cale liked what she was offering. He grabbed her and yanked her to him to kiss her.

"That should keep you 'til I get back." He stuffed some money down her bodice. "Make sure you're ready for me."

She smiled up at him. "I'll be ready, big guy. You'll see. You hurry back now, you hear?" She gave him a bold wink as he left the saloon.

Though she hadn't gotten him upstairs, she had gotten some cash out of her ploy, and that pleased her for the time being. She went on to tease some of the other customers, knowing she probably had a good half hour before Cale would return.

Cale was drunk and in a troubled mood as he made his way down the street to the stable. He'd found himself thinking about Jim again, and worrying about him. When they'd parted on the trail, everything had seemed fine, but after all this time without any sign of him at all, Cale wasn't so sure. The thought that his good friend might be dead angered him, but he knew there was nothing he could do but wait and hope Jim was still out there somewhere, trying to catch up with them. He thought about riding back in the direction Jim would be coming to see if he could find him, but there was no telling just where his friend might have ridden.

Cale reached the stable and took a look around. He found their horses were in good condition and being well taken care of. The owner of the stable wasn't anywhere to be seen, and that was fine with Cale. He hadn't wanted to talk to anybody, he'd just wanted to get away from all the noise in the saloon for a while.

As he started back toward the saloon, he heard what sounded like a fight going on in the alley behind the stable. He didn't know who was back there, but he'd thought he'd take a look just to see what was going on. He always liked a good fight.

And that was just the decision Grant had hoped the outlaw would make.

Grant and Dusty had reached Flat Rock an hour before and had checked the town out carefully and quietly. Grant had spotted the outlaws through the saloon window and had known this was going to be the night that Les Jackson, Cale Pierce and Ugly Joe Williams were brought to justice.

He'd made sure he and Dusty stayed out of sight while they waited to see what the gang was going to do. He couldn't have been more pleased when he saw Cale leave the saloon and head off down the street. He and Dusty had stayed back, watching the outlaw's every move and then hid in an alley when Cale went into the stable. As soon as the outlaw emerged, the two of them started a ruckus that could not be missed.

When Cale started down the alley, Grant was ready. He staggered toward the outlaw, eyeing him in the dark of the alley.

"What are you doing?" Grant challenged. "Looking for trouble?"

Cale was used to dealing with drunks, so he wasn't the least bit worried about being able to hold his own with this one. "I'm always looking for trouble," Cale said arrogantly, believing he was about to have himself a real good time.

"Well, you found it," Grant announced as he looked up and aimed his gun straight at the other man.

The dim light in the alley glinted off a Texas Ranger badge and Cale knew he was in real trouble. He started to go for his gun, but another voice spoke out from behind the Ranger.

"Don't even think about it—"

Cale thought the voice sounded vaguely familiar, but he had no time to worry about that. He was desperately trying to figure out how to get away from the Ranger. He was furious with himself for going into the alley now, but he didn't move, knowing he'd be dead in an instant if he tried to draw his gun.

"You're under arrest, Pierce," Grant told him. "Get down on the ground, facedown, and don't try anything. I'm taking you in. Whether it's dead or alive is your choice."

Cale did as he'd been ordered. He wasn't totally without hope, though, for he was sure Les and Ugly Joe would free him.

Grant didn't trust the outlaw at all. He clubbed him with his gun, knocking him unconscious, and then quickly tied him up and gagged him. He checked Pierce's pockets and found a key to a hotel room.

"Looks like this is where they're staying," he said, tossing the key to Dusty.

Dusty had been staying out of sight, armed with

her own gun, keeping lookout for Grant just in case the other two outlaws showed up. She deftly caught the key. "What are we going to do with him?"

"Watch him for a minute. I'm going to get the stable hand."

"Do you think it's safe to trust anyone in this town?" she worried.

"If the stable hand knows what's good for him, he'll help us," Grant said, his expression grim. "Stay here. I'll be right back."

Grant made his way into the deserted stable and knocked on the door to the small back room.

A sleepy-looking older man threw open the door and glared at Grant. "What do you—"

And then he saw the Ranger badge. His eyes widened.

"You're a Ranger?"

"That's right, and I need your help."

"Anything—anything you need—" the man quickly agreed, knowing better than to defy a Ranger.

"I was hoping you'd see things that way. Come with me." Grant started back out to the alley. "What's your name?"

"I'm Gus."

"I'm Ranger Spencer."

They made their way to where Dusty was standing guard. Grant was pleased to see that Cale was still unconscious. He didn't want any more trouble out of the outlaw.

"Help me carry him back to your room. I want you to keep him locked up for me until we come for him."

"What did he do?" Gus looked from the tied-up man to the lawman.

"He's part of the Jackson gang. We're taking him in."

"The Jackson gang?" Gus looked frightened. "They're here in Flat Rock?"

"Not for much longer," Grant assured him.

"I'm glad you're here, Ranger Spencer. We're not the most peaceful town around, but we don't need their kind here. And who you got with you?"

"This is 'the kid,'" he answered, offering no more.

"Oh—" Gus could tell the Ranger had said all he was going to say.

Grant lifted the outlaw by the shoulders while Gus took his feet.

"Go see if the street's empty," Grant ordered Dusty. He didn't want Les or Ugly Joe to get wind of what was going on.

Dusty hurried ahead to check things out.

"It's clear," she called back quietly.

Grant and the stable hand quickly carried Cale into the stable and straight to the back room.

"Where do you want him?" Grant asked.

"Put him on the floor. He don't deserve no better than that," Gus answered. He'd heard how murderous the Jackson gang was, and he was going to make sure this man's killing days were over. When the Ranger came back, the outlaw was going to be right where the lawman had left him.

Grant lowered Cale to the floor, then quickly checked his gag to make sure it was tight, as well as the ropes that bound his wrists and ankles.

"I appreciate your help," he told Gus.

Gus nodded. "When are you coming back for him?"

"As soon as we bring down the other two," Grant said, taking one last look at the outlaw and then leaving the room. "Make sure this room stays locked. I don't want any surprises."

"I will. You have my word on it."

Grant and Dusty quickly left the stable, heading for the hotel.

"You did a good job back there," Grant told her, impressed that she'd been steady and had shown no fear. "But it's going to get worse from here on out, so be ready."

"I will be." Dusty had always thought Grant was smart, and after watching him in action, she knew he was a force to be reckoned with. If anyone was going to bring down Les Jackson, it would be Grant, and she was going to be right there with him. She was, after all, his partner now—he'd said so. "It looks like your friend Frank didn't get here ahead of us."

"I know. I've been wondering where he is. He's a good man at tracking, and now I'm starting to get a little worried."

"You think something might have happened to him?" She looked over at Grant as they moved slowly through the darkened streets of Flat Rock.

"I intend to find out."

She heard the edge of tension in his voice and didn't say anything more.

Grant stopped about a block away from the hotel

and drew Dusty back into the shadows of the deserted street to plan their next move.

"I'm going to take a look around the hotel. The way you climbed in my window back in Gold Canyon has given me an idea. I'm going to see if I can figure out a way to surprise each outlaw in his room. If we can do that, it'll be a lot easier to take them."

"Do you want me to come with you?"

"Not right now. Just stay back here out of sight. I won't be long."

Dusty didn't like the idea of Grant going off by himself. She was afraid someone might ambush him. She realized then as she watched him walk away that in spite of the anger she'd felt when he'd left her behind, she did love him. Accepting the truth of her feelings wasn't easy, but she had to admit he was an honorable and strong man, and his motive for leaving her behind had been to protect her and keep her safe.

Dusty found herself actually smiling in the darkness. He'd said it. She was his "partner" now, and she liked the sound of that. She kept her hand resting on her sidearm, and as she awaited his return, she said a prayer for his safety.

Grant focused solely on what he had to do. Les and Ugly Joe were still on the loose, and he was going to put an end to their killing ways tonight. He moved down a side street and circled around behind the hotel. It frustrated him to discover that there was no covered porch on the back of the building, so he and Dusty wouldn't be sneaking in through a window.

Grant went back to find Dusty. He knew what he had to do. They would go up to Cale's room and wait for the other two to show up at the hotel. Then he would make his move. He couldn't afford any mistakes when he was dealing with Les Jackson, not even if the man was drunk. Jackson's reputation as a fast and deadly gun was well-known. Grant knew he had to be faster—and deadlier.

He was glad Dusty had listened to him. He found her right where he'd told her to stay.

"We're not going to be climbing in any windows," he told her. "There's no way to get to the second floor."

Dusty was disappointed, but knew they could figure something out. "I'm ready. Let's get this over with." She was looking forward to seeing Jackson pay for what he'd done.

Grant was tense and ready for action as he looked down at her. "So am I."

Chapter Twenty-one

It was late when Ugly Joe threw his poker hand down in the middle of the table in total disgust. He angrily pushed his chair away from the table and stood up. This was the first night he'd lost at gambling since arriving in Flat Rock.

"You quitting?" one of the men asked, disappointed. He'd liked taking the ugly stranger's money.

"You're damned right, I'm quitting. I'm done," Ugly Joe snarled, staggering away.

"Don't forget to come back tomorrow night—" the man joked, but he quickly shut up when Ugly Joe turned back and gave him a deadly look.

Ugly Joe glanced at Les, who was still sitting at the table. "You coming?"

"Yeah. I reckon it's quitting time." Les finished off his whiskey and got up, too.

"We'll be back tomorrow. You boys be ready. We're gonna win back what we lost tonight."

"We'll be right here," the other gamblers assured them.

* * *

In the dark of Cale's room, Grant and Dusty waited tensely for the other two outlaws to show up. When they'd come into the hotel, the clerk hadn't been at the desk, so Dusty had quickly checked the sign-in book to see what rooms the outlaws were staying in. She'd had some practice sneaking a look at hotel registries, so Grant had known she was good at it.

They'd kept quiet once they'd reached Cale's room, not wanting to miss the outlaws' approach in the hallway. Before too long, they heard loud footsteps outside in the hall and the raucous sound of drunken laughter.

"There are some benefits to laying low like this," Ugly Joe told Les as they reached the top of the stairs at the hotel.

"Yeah? Like what?"

"Like sleeping in a real bed at night."

"You're right about that."

"Too bad we ain't got no willing women with us, but I guess we can't have everything."

"There's a few over at the saloon who'd take care of you," Les said. "For a price—"

They both laughed.

"Yeah, they'd do just about anything for the right price."

"I wonder what happened to Cale?" Les looked toward the door to Cale's room and saw no light coming from under the door.

"I'm sure we'll find out in the morning."

Ugly Joe stopped at his room.

"You got any plans for tomorrow?" he asked Les.

Les looked at him, his expression a bit dark. "Yeah, I got plans. I'm going to win my money back from those boys."

"I like the way you think, Les. We'll plan on that," Ugly Joe said as he unlocked his own door and went in.

Les went on to his room at the far end of the hall.

Ugly Joe stumbled inside. He usually wouldn't have worried about keeping the door locked, but the gang had split up the haul from the stage robbery, and there was no way to keep all that money on him all the time.

Lurching drunkenly about the room, he managed to shut and lock the door behind him. He went to light the lamp and left it burning low as he sat down on the bed to take off his boots. He wasn't even worried about getting out of his clothes tonight. He just wanted to lie down and pass out. Ugly Joe stood up for a minute to unbuckle his gun belt, and after tossing it on the table at one side of the room, he stretched out on the bed. He thought about getting back up and putting out the lamp, but thought it would take too much energy. He closed his eyes, ready to relax.

When Grant heard Les and Ugly Joe in the hall, he knew he'd made the right decision about waiting in Cale's room for the outlaws' return. He hadn't expected both of them to show up at the same time. Had he and Dusty been waiting in Les's or

Ugly Joe's room to take one of them by surprise, they would have had to deal with both men together.

Grant went to Dusty.

"Ugly Joe's in the room next door, so here's what we're going to do—" he began in a whisper, then went on to explain his quickly conceived plan.

Her eyes widened at the brilliance of his idea, especially after what they'd just overheard the outlaws saying in the hallway.

"How soon?"

"We'll give it a few more minutes and let them get settled in."

She nodded, more than ready to take action.

Ugly Joe was just about to fall asleep when he heard a soft knock at the door.

"Yeah? Who is it?" he mumbled, thinking it was probably Les and wondering what the other man wanted.

Ugly Joe was surprised when a low, enticing feminine voice came to him through the door.

"Hey, handsome, I got some room service for you— Les told me I should take real good care of you—"

Ugly Joe couldn't imagine how Les had gotten back to the saloon fast enough to send one of the girls to him, but he wasn't going to question his luck.

He sat up and slowly got to his feet.

"Hold on, honey— Don't go nowhere—" he called out in a slurred voice. "I'm coming—"

He unlocked the door and opened it, only to get the shock of his life.

He was expecting a scantily dressed saloon girl, ready to meet his needs.

Instead, he found himself staring down the barrel of a gun.

"What the—?"

Ugly Joe was so stunned, he stood unmoving for a second, and his slight hesitation gave Grant just the opportunity he needed. In one move, Grant stepped boldly into the room. He'd hoped to be able to take down Ugly Joe as easily as he'd gotten Cale, but he wasn't so lucky. The outlaw tackled him, and they grappled together on the floor.

Dusty knew that any undue disturbance would bring Les running from down the hall, so she quickly came inside, and shut and locked the door behind her.

The fight was a fierce one. Desperate to escape, Ugly Joe gave no thought to anything but survival.

Dusty knew Grant could handle him, but she wanted to help. This was one of the men who'd killed her father. She holstered her gun and ran to the washstand. She grabbed up the pitcher, then turned back to the fight. The first chance she got, she smashed the pitcher over the outlaw's head. The pitcher shattered, and she watched in satisfaction as Ugly Joe collapsed, unconscious and bleeding.

Grant quickly knelt beside the outlaw and rolled him over.

"How is he?" Dusty asked, drawing her gun again. She wanted to be ready, just in case.

"He's out," Grant said in disgust.

"Good."

He got to his feet and looked at Dusty. "You're pretty handy with a pitcher."

"Thanks." She felt confident as she stared down at Ugly Joe where he lay bloodied on the hotel room floor. The thought came to her then that her father would have been proud of her. Tears threatened, but she forced the painful emotion from her. There was no time for that now. They had another outlaw to bring in.

Grant quickly tied up Ugly Joe with a length of rope he'd brought along. He gagged the outlaw, too.

So far, so good.

While Grant was tying up the outlaw, Dusty swept away the broken pieces of pitcher and checked Ugly Joe's gear to make sure there were no knives or other sharp objects that he might be able to reach if he regained consciousness while they went after Les. She remembered her own efforts with the sharp rock back at the gang's campsite. She wasn't going to give him any chance to break loose and escape. She quickly unloaded his rifle and then went to get the outlaw's revolver. She stuck it in her waistband, just in case she needed an extra gun.

Ready for more trouble, Dusty looked toward Grant as he finished with Ugly Joe. He looked so rugged and so in control. She wanted to go to him and hug him. She wanted to stay in the safe haven of his arms, but she knew better.

There was no time for any emotion right now.

They were about to face down Les Jackson.

Grant was unaware of her thoughts. He was only concerned with acting quickly enough to catch Jackson off guard.

"We need to move fast. I don't think anybody heard us," Grant said, "but I don't want to take any chances."

The final moment had now come in what seemed like his endless pursuit of the killers.

He wanted Les Jackson, and he was going to get him.

Grant saw no need for subtlety in dealing with the cold-blooded killer. They knew Les was in his room, and with any luck, he'd passed out by now. His time of running free was about to come to an end.

"There's no playing with Jackson," he told Dusty. "I'm going to kick the door in and go right after him."

"What do you want me to do?" she asked, ready to back him up.

"Just stay down and watch the hallway."

"I can do that," she assured him.

Grant saw the fierceness in her expression and knew she was ready for whatever might come their way. A part of him wanted to kiss her right then, but he controlled the urge. There could be only one thing on his mind right now, and that was getting Jackson.

"Let's go."

Dusty followed Grant from Ugly Joe's room, and she was relieved to find it was quiet in the hall. No one had been disturbed by the fight with Ugly Joe. They moved silently down the hall to the room they knew was Jackson's.

They both drew their guns, and Grant's gaze met Dusty's one last time for a long moment. Then he kicked the door with all his might and threw himself into the room, tumbling down low.

Drunk as he was, Les hadn't even bothered to light the lamp. He'd just stretched out on his bed fully clothed and had gone sound asleep. The sound of the door crashing open brought him instantly awake and upright in the bed. He went for his gun and started blindly firing rounds in the darkness.

Grant had been ready for him. Though the only light in the room was from the dim light of the hall, Grant came to his knees and got off a shot at Les that found its mark. He heard Les scream and fall off the bed on the far side. Grant didn't know if he'd killed the outlaw leader, so he moved silently closer to check. He found Les unmoving on the floor and reached down to grab the gun that had fallen from the outlaw's grip.

Dusty was a little frightened by all the gunfire, and people were coming out into the hall, looking around. "Is it all right, Grant?" she asked.

"Yes," he answered tightly. He quickly lit the lamp on the table and went to the doorway. He stepped into the hall, his gun and Jackson's still in hand, so everyone could see his badge. "I'm a Texas Ranger. Go on back to your rooms."

Everyone hurried to do just as he'd ordered.

Grant left the door open so he could keep track

of what was going on in the hall. He told Dusty to stay by the door and then went to the far side of the bed to check Jackson more carefully. He wasn't sure if he'd killed him or if the outlaw was just unconscious. When he rolled the injured man over, Jackson groaned. Grant dragged him out from behind the bed to check his wound. It was a chest wound, and bleeding heavily. Grant could tell the wound was serious.

"He's alive?" Dusty asked, coming to stand by him.

"For now. Let's get him on the bed."

The two of them lifted the outlaw and laid him on the bed. Grant took the blanket and used it to try to stop the bleeding.

"Do you think he'll make it?" Dusty wondered as she went back to guarding the door.

"I don't know."

Les was conscious, but he didn't want the Ranger to know that. He'd been shot before, but never like this. He knew he was dying, and he didn't have long.

Les had managed to open one eye just enough to catch sight of the Ranger's badge, and it infuriated him. He'd recognized Dusty's voice when they'd spoken to each other, and his anger at being outsmarted grew. He had to get even—somehow.

Les knew then what he was going to do. If he was going to die, he was going to take one of them with him. He still had his single-shot derringer in his pocket, and since he didn't have long to live, he was going to use it now.

When Grant turned away to get a towel from the washstand, Les knew it was his only chance to exact his revenge. He drew the gun and rolled slightly to get a shot off at Dusty, who was standing by the door.

Grant had caught sight of a movement on the bed and turned just as Les was getting ready to fire.

"Dusty! Look out!"

Grant threw himself at her to shove her out of the way just as Les got off his one and only shot. The bullet winged Grant's upper arm, but it didn't stop him. He drew his own gun and fired, killing the outlaw instantly.

"Grant!" Dusty saw that he'd been hit and rushed to him.

Grant sat up and looked to her. "Are you all right? You weren't hurt?"

"No, I'm fine. You saved me," she said, kneeling by his side to check his arm.

Grant looked over at his wound and knew it wasn't serious.

Dusty pulled out her own handkerchief and bound his arm. "That should hold it until we have time to clean it properly."

They both stood up, and in that instant, Dusty couldn't help herself. She wrapped her arms around him and closed her eyes, burying her face against his chest as her tears began to fall.

"Thank God, it wasn't serious—" She could feel the tension in him as she held him close.

He held her for a moment, then gently took her arms from around him. He looked down at her, his expression grave as he realized how close Jackson had come to shooting her. "You could have been killed."

"No. Not with you here," she said, remembering Francie calling him her guardian angel. She lifted one hand to caress his cheek, knowing just how deep her love for him was.

Grant gave her another gentle hug and then put her from him. There was a lot he had to say to her, but this was not the time or the place.

He turned to look at Jackson where he lay dead on the bed. Even on his death bed, the man had thought only of killing. The realization sickened Grant and he turned away.

"We've got a lot to accomplish tonight. I'll take Ugly Joe down to the stable while you go get the undertaker. There's no law here in Flat Rock, so after we finish taking care of Jackson, we'll take the other two back to Gold Canyon and turn them over to the sheriff there."

Dusty knew it was going to be a difficult trip, but they'd do it. "How soon do you want to leave?"

"At dawn."

Chapter Twenty-two

Cale had regained consciousness, but was unable to move or make a sound as he lay bound in the back room of the stable. He waited there alone for a long time and then he finally heard the door being unlocked. He watched carefully to see who was coming in, and soon learned it was the man he'd seen working at the stable earlier that day. He grunted and squirmed, trying to get the fellow's attention, but the man just gave him a cold, hard look.

"Don't get any ideas about me setting you free. That Texas Ranger will be back, and he's going to take you in." Gus was satisfied when he saw the look of fear that shone in the outlaw's eyes. "You'd better be scared," he taunted. He'd heard all about this deadly gang of gunmen, and he was glad that the law had finally caught up with them. "He's facing down your partners right now, but he'll be back. That's for sure."

Gus sat down in the chair across the small room from where the gunman lay on the floor, planning to keep a close eye on him.

It wasn't too much longer before a knock came

at the door. Gus quickly went to answer it. "Who is it?"

"Ranger Spencer," Grant answered quietly.

Gus didn't hesitate. He unlocked the door and was not surprised to find Grant half dragging another man with him. The other outlaw had his wrists bound behind him, and he was gagged, too. Grant shoved Ugly Joe down on the floor next to Cale and quickly bound his legs, too.

"You got 'em all?" Gus asked, impressed with the lawman.

Grant nodded. "Jackson's dead."

When Cale and Ugly Joe both heard the news about Les, they were shocked. Les was the fastest gun around. They didn't know how this Ranger had done it, but they knew they were in serious trouble. Their last and only hope of freedom would be if Jim showed up right now.

"Weren't there four men riding in the gang?" Gus asked, remembering all he'd heard about them.

"That's right. I caught up with Jim Harper a few towns back. Killed him in a shoot-out."

"You're one fine Ranger."

Grant looked at the stable man, his expression serious. "I'm just doing my job."

Cale and Ugly Joe were furious to know this Ranger had killed Jim, too. The only solace they had was that they'd killed the other Ranger, and they intended to brag about that the first chance they got.

"Looks like you got winged there," Gus remarked. "Let me take a look at that arm."

Grant didn't say anything as the stable man tore

back his shirtsleeve and set to quickly cleaning up and doctoring the graze with the medicine he had stored there in a small dresser. Gus bandaged the wound.

"I don't think that'll give you any trouble."

"At least it's not my shooting arm," Grant said with a half smile. "Thanks, Gus."

"Where's the kid?" Gus asked.

"Getting our gear ready. We'll be riding out at first light. Did they stable their horses here?"

"I got all three of them," he responded.

"Keep whichever one you want, but I'll need two to transport these men to Gold Canyon."

"I'll have them ready for you at sunup," Gus offered. "Do you and the kid want to bed down back here for a couple of hours? That way you can keep an eye on these two while you get some rest. I can sleep out in one of the stalls."

"That's real kind of you," Grant said in appreciation. He'd been wondering how he and Dusty were going to get any rest tonight. As it was, he still wasn't going to get much, but at least Dusty could get in a few hours of sleep.

"You need anything, just let me know," Gus said as he left Grant alone with his prisoners.

Grant looked down at Cale and Ugly Joe to find them watching him, their expressions hate filled, and he knew he couldn't let himself relax until they were safely locked up in Gold Canyon.

"You boys might as well try to get some rest, too. You're in for some long, hard riding in the morning," he said.

Just as he'd finished speaking, Dusty came into the room. She stopped inside the door and stared down in disgust at the captured outlaws. "Gus said we were staying in here for now?"

"That's right."

"He fixed your arm?" She noticed the bandage.

"Yes. It was nothing serious. If you want to sleep for a while, I'll keep watch," Grant offered, gesturing toward the small bed against the wall. He could tell she was exhausted.

"I'll try," she agreed. She knew they had to be ready for anything over the next two days while they transported the killers to the jail.

Cale and Ugly Joe were even more furious to see Dusty with the Ranger. They had no idea how she'd come to be riding with a Texas Ranger, but they knew now they'd been fools not to stay on her trail when she'd escaped from them that night. None of this would have happened if they hadn't given up trying to find her. Now, she was the one who'd tracked them down. Ugly Joe, in particular, was humiliated that she'd caught him so off guard up in his hotel room. He wished he'd ignored Les's warning and gone ahead and raped her when they were first riding out of Canyon Springs. That was what she deserved. He hoped he could manage to get free somehow and take his revenge, but if nothing else he had the satisfaction of knowing they'd killed her daddy and the other Ranger.

Dusty curled up in the narrow bed, facing the wall so she wouldn't be looking at the outlaws, while Grant settled into the only chair in the room.

The last few hours of the night passed slowly. Grant was glad when he saw that both outlaws had fallen asleep. He didn't let his guard down, though. Glancing over toward the bed, he thought it looked like Dusty had fallen asleep, and he was glad. She needed the rest.

As Grant watched Dusty, he knew the time was coming when he was going to have to decide what he was going to do with her. He loved her. He knew he'd met his match in the feisty tomboy, and he wasn't going to let her go. He had been relentless in tracking down the Jackson gang, and he planned to be just as relentless in winning her hand.

The memory of Miss Gertrude handing Justine over to him at the dance in Canyon Springs played in his mind, and Grant realized that night seemed like a lifetime ago after all they'd been through. He found himself looking forward to seeing her wearing a fancy gown again, and he definitely was looking forward to holding her close—

Grant had to force his thoughts back to the reality before him.

He had Ugly Joe Williams and Cale Pierce to bring in.

The rest would have to wait.

Grant tore his gaze away from Dusty and concentrated on staying awake.

It was just before sunup when Grant woke Dusty and then left the room to find Gus already up and waiting for him. Grant was surprised to find the stable hand had gotten them a hot breakfast.

"That was real nice of you, Gus," Grant told him.

"My girlie friend is the cook over at the saloon."

"From the way it smells, I'd say she's a good cook."

"How do you want to do this?" Dusty asked, joining them.

"You go ahead and eat, while I see about getting those two ready to ride."

"All right."

"As soon as they eat a bite, we'll ride out."

"You eat something, too," Dusty told him.

"Don't worry. I will."

He went to rouse his prisoners. He took off their gags and made short order of tying their hands in front of them, then untying their ankles. When they finally joined Dusty and Gus, the two outlaws didn't say a thing. They just gorged themselves on the biscuits and bacon and hot coffee.

Grant took Gus aside to talk to him privately for a minute, and it wasn't too much later that they returned with two lengths of chain attached to some metal cuffs.

"This will work," Gus told Grant, and over the snarling protests of the prisoners, he quickly chained their wrists together in front of them. "That'll hold 'em until you get to Gold Canyon." He looked at the angry outlaws. "You might as well get used to these chains. You'll be wearing them while you're in the pen."

Ugly Joe and Cale knew he was right, and the thought of ending up on the chain gangs terrified and unnerved them. They said nothing more.

Dusty was glad that Grant had thought of the

chains. She'd been on edge, worrying that their captives would figure out a way to escape just like she had.

With the prisoners now securely restrained, Grant and Gus wasted no time getting the horses saddled. It was just getting light out as they mounted up.

"I can't thank you enough, Gus."

"Glad to help, Ranger Spencer."

The two men shook hands.

"Good luck to you," Gus bid.

Grant was holding the reins to their horses, and he noticed that Ugly Joe and Cale were watching them real carefully.

"Don't even think about trying anything," Grant ordered. "Like I told you before—I'm taking you in—dead or alive. It's your choice from here on."

Cale and Ugly Joe stayed silent as Dusty and Grant rode out of Flat Rock, leading the outlaws' horses.

Keeping pace with Grant, Dusty felt a warm glow of accomplishment

They had done it—

They'd caught Les Jackson and his men.

It was the moment she'd been living for. The capture of the gang put an end to the nightmare her life had become. She knew she should have been thrilled that it was over, but, in truth, as she faced her future for the first time, she felt only a great emptiness within.

She had no idea what she was going to do. Her need for revenge had kept her going since her father's death, but now—

Now, she faced the reality of her existence—
She had nothing.
She had no family.

It took all the willpower she could muster to keep up a brave face. She wasn't about to give in to her heartache now. She couldn't be weak. She had to stay strong. They had to finish the trek to Gold Canyon with Ugly Joe and Cale. Only when she saw them locked up would she allow herself to consider what she was going to do with the rest of her life.

Dusty thought of Francie then and missed her friend desperately. She wondered how Francie was, and if her friend thought she was dead. She was certain the posse from town had never come near to catching up to the Jackson gang, so there was no way for Francie and her parents or Miss Gertrude to know what had happened to her. The thought of seeing her friends again heartened her, and she found she couldn't wait for the trek to Gold Canyon to be over.

Chapter Twenty-three

Ugly Joe and Cale looked at the Ranger and Dusty as they sat opposite the campfire from them late that night. Neither outlaw had said much during the long ride, but now that they were settled in, Ugly Joe and Cale were ready to taunt the lawman with what they knew about the missing Ranger.

"Yeah, Les and me did a real good job," Ugly Joe bragged to Cale, grinning broadly at him.

"I'll say you did," Cale agreed. "Why, the way you and Les gunned down that other Ranger— That was some fine shooting."

They both noticed how Grant tensed at their words, and they smiled even more. They wanted to make him miserable.

"Yes, it was. He'd been trailing us after we split up, and Les had had enough. He wanted that Ranger out of the way, so we were waiting for him up in a canyon near Eagle Ridge," Ugly Joe went on. "I always knew Les was a good shot, but that day— I'm telling you that Ranger had no idea we were hiding up there, ready for him. Best I could tell, Les got him in the head. Then his horse bucked him off and threw him down the canyon. We had some real cause for celebrating—"

It wasn't often Grant lost control, but when he looked up at Ugly Joe and saw the smug grin on the outlaw's face, his temper exploded. He threw himself at the outlaw and pinned him to the ground, his forearm pressed against the other man's throat.

"What did you say?" Grant demanded harshly.

Ugly Joe was half choking, but he still managed to smile up at him and sneer, "You heard me. Me and Les ambushed the Ranger that was following us. We killed him, and we was real glad we did."

Shocked by what had happened, Dusty leaped up and drew her gun, just in case the outlaws tried to break free.

Grant glared down at Ugly Joe, thinking of Frank being ambushed and killed by these cold-blooded gunmen. Fury, rage and devastation filled him.

For an instant, Grant wanted to exact justice right then and there.

He didn't want to wait for a judge and jury.

He pressed down harder on the outlaw's throat. There was no doubt he would feel no sorrow over Ugly Joe Williams's death, but somehow, he managed to restrain his fierce, feral need for revenge. It wasn't easy, but he drew back in disgust. In short order, he quickly gagged both prisoners again to silence their taunts, then got up and moved away.

"I'll be back—" he told Dusty in a low voice, his face bleak with sorrow as he walked off into the night.

Dusty understood his need to be alone. She backed a little farther away from the two prisoners, but kept her gun trained on them. Even though they were restrained, she didn't trust them for a minute.

Grant moved some distance away to stare out across the darkened land. Frank was out there somewhere. A great resolution filled him, and he knew once he'd turned the outlaws over to the law in Gold Canyon, he would go find his friend. It wouldn't be easy to locate Frank's body after all this time, but he had to try. He could do no less for his partner.

When Grant returned to the camp, he was glad to see that the prisoners had bedded down.

Dusty had been watching for Grant. When she saw him coming out of the darkness, her breath caught in her throat. He looked powerful and commanding, and his expression had hardened, revealing no emotion. She knew he was a man on a mission, and nothing was going to stop him from seeing these two men brought to justice.

"I'll take first watch," Dusty offered. "You get some rest."

"All right. Wake me in an hour or two," he said as he sought what comfort he could find on his bedroll and closed his eyes.

Dusty sat down a short distance away from the campfire, determined to keep a close watch on the prisoners. She was armed and ready for anything they might try. She planned to let Grant sleep longer than he'd told her, knowing he needed all the rest he could get, but he awoke on his own and took over so she could get some sleep, too.

At dawn, they were on their way, planning to reach Gold Canyon by midday.

They rode into town just after noon and brought the two outlaws to the jail, where they turned them over to Sheriff Becker along with what was left of the money they'd stolen. After the sheriff had made sure Ugly Joe Williams and Cale Pierce were securely locked up, Grant and Dusty had told him all that had happened in Flat Rock.

"I'm proud of what you've done," the sheriff told them. "You've saved a lot of innocent lives by stopping Les Jackson and his men. What are you going to do next, Ranger Spencer?"

Grant's expression darkened. "I'm going to wire my captain and let him know I've put an end to the Jackson gang, and then I'm going to ride for Eagle Ridge and see if I can find Frank."

Dusty had known Grant was deeply troubled by the news of his partner's death, but she hadn't expected him to ride for Eagle Ridge. She didn't know what she'd expected to happen, but she realized now they would soon be parting company. She supposed he would want to put her on a stage and send her back to Canyon Springs so he could be done with her. All the emotions she'd fought so hard to keep under control were threatening to overwhelm her, and she knew she wouldn't be able to keep the tears away much longer.

Fortunately, she was sure neither man was aware of her thoughts.

Sheriff Becker looked at Grant. "I understand what you're feeling. I don't know if I'd believe anything they told me either."

"I intend to find out what really happened to Frank."

"Well, if there's anything I can do for you while you're here in town, just let me know," Becker offered.

"Thanks, Sheriff," Grant said.

As he and Dusty started from his office, Ugly Joe and Cale yelled out at them from their jail cells. "We ain't done with you!"

Grant moved back so they could see him as he responded harshly, "Oh, yes, you are. Get used to seeing those bars. You're going to be spending a lot of time behind them."

He turned his back and walked away from the killers, ignoring the foul language they hurled at him. He was glad to know they would never be free again to hurt anyone else.

Grant and Dusty stepped outside to stand on the sidewalk. Grant knew what he wanted to do—he wanted to get Dusty alone and kiss her. This would be the first time they would be alone together without the threat of the outlaw gang hanging over them, but first he had to send the telegram to his captain and let him know everything that had happened and the news about Frank.

"Let's get some rooms at the hotel, and then I'll go send that telegram," he said.

"All right," Dusty replied briefly, trying hard to keep her emotions in check.

Grant thought she was quiet just because she was tired.

"I think we've been in this room before," he said drolly as he went upstairs with her to see her safely to the room the clerk had given her.

"Yes, we have." Dusty realized then that her room was the same one he'd had the night she'd caught up with him. She paused to look up at him as she opened the door to go in. "Which room is yours?"

"I'm right next door," he told her. "Do you need anything else?"

"No," she answered.

"Then I'll be back after I take care of our horses and send the wire," he told her.

Dusty went into her room and tossed her gear on the chair. She happened to look up and saw her reflection in the mirror. It wasn't the first time she'd been taken aback by her appearance, but as she stared at her image, a great sadness welled up inside of her. She hadn't meant to lose control so quickly, but her broken heart overwhelmed her.

Throwing herself across the bed, Dusty gave in to the heartache that she'd borne for all this time. There could be no more hiding from the truth. She was truly alone in the world. She wept, her sorrow leaving her devastated and vulnerable.

Dusty knew Grant had watched over her during their hunt for the outlaws, but that had only been because he'd been forced to take her along. She

believed if he'd had his way, she would have taken
the stage back to Canyon Springs, and he would
never have seen her again. Dusty honestly believed
when he returned to the hotel that afternoon, he
would be ready to put her on another stage and go
his own way. He certainly didn't need her anymore.
They'd accomplished their goal. They'd caught the
Jackson gang.

Grant had gone into his hotel room to leave his
saddlebags and rifle, and had just started back down
the hall when he heard a strange, muffled sound
coming from Dusty's room. Fearing something was
wrong, he stopped and threw the door open.

It hadn't even occurred to Dusty to lock the door.
After all, Gold Canyon was a safe town. She was unnerved when the door flew open so unexpectedly.
She forced herself to look up from where she was
lying on the bed, and found Grant standing over her.

"Dusty? What is it?"

He pushed the door shut behind him and sat
down beside her on the bed, lifting her onto his lap
and holding her against his chest. She was trembling as she buried her face against him and continued to weep. He suddenly realized as he cradled
her so protectively in his arms, just how delicate
and fragile she truly was.

"Dusty, darling, it's all right. Everything is all
right now," he crooned, trying to calm her.

"No—no, it's not—" she managed in an emotion-
choked voice.

"You're safe, darling," he said quietly. "The gang
will never hurt you or anyone else ever again."

"You don't understand," she said, keeping her face hidden against him.

"Tell me—"

"It's over— My life is over—" She lifted her head to look up at him.

He could see the pain that was devastating her. "No, it's not—"

"My father is dead. I miss him. We only had each other after my mother died, and now— Now, I'm alone—"

Grant understood how she was feeling more than she would ever know as he remembered his own father's death. He carefully reached up to wipe some tears from her cheek. "You're not alone, Dusty— You've got me—"

She was stunned by his words and could only stare at him in total confusion.

"Dusty, I love you. I've never known another woman like you, and I want you to marry me," he said softly, holding her gaze.

"What—?" she whispered, not believing what she was hearing.

"You'll never be alone again, Dusty. I'll be with you always. Marry me, darling."

Ever so gently, he bent to kiss her. It was a loving exchange, and conveyed better than any words what he was feeling for her.

When the kiss ended, Dusty drew back to look up at him.

Grant gazed down at her, unable to read her expression. He had no idea what she was thinking, and for a moment, he worried that she didn't feel the same way about him.

"Oh, Grant—" she said, starting to cry again. "I love you, too. I think I have ever since we danced that night in town—"

At her words, he gathered her to him again and kissed her deeply.

"So you'll marry me?" he asked, smiling down at her.

Dusty was half crying, half laughing as she answered. "Yes. I'll marry you, Grant Spencer."

She wrapped her arms around him and clung to him, savoring the pure joy of the moment. She had thought she was alone in the world, but she'd been wrong. She had Grant.

"How do you want to do this? Do you want to wait until we go back to Canyon Springs?"

She answered quickly. "No. There's no reason to wait. Without my papa there to give me away—"

The thought saddened Dusty, and Grant felt the change in her. He bent again to press a sweet kiss to her cheek.

"Do you want to get married now? We could see if there's a justice of the peace in town willing to do the job."

She looked down at what she was wearing. Her pants and shirt were a far cry from a white satin wedding gown. "But my clothes—"

"Dusty, I love you no matter what you're wearing, but if you want to go buy yourself a dress to get married in, that's fine with me."

"Really?"

"Really." He kissed her one last time. "I'll go take care of my business and see what I can find out about having a wedding. I'll meet you back here."

"I'll be waiting."

Chapter Twenty-four

The clerk in the telegraph office looked up at the Ranger after he finished sending his message. "I'd already heard the news about your bringing in the Jackson gang. Word travels fast here in Gold Canyon. Good work, Ranger Spencer."

"I'm just glad they're not running free anymore."

"So is everybody else in Texas," the clerk told him.

"Thanks. I'm staying over at the hotel if you hear back." Grant gave the man his room number.

"If I get a response, I'll run it right over to you."

"I appreciate that. I did have one other question," Grant began.

"What can I help you with?"

"Is there a justice of the peace in town?"

The clerk looked a little puzzled as he answered. "Yes, right down the block. His name's George Arnold."

Grant smiled for the first time. "Good. I've got a wedding to plan."

"You're getting married?"

"As soon as I can arrange it."

"Congratulations. You're a lucky man."

Grant went quiet for a minute, thinking of how close Dusty had come to being killed by Les Jackson at the hotel. He said, "Yes, I am."

Grant left the telegraph office and headed down the street to meet with the justice of the peace.

As soon as Grant had left her, Dusty thought about taking a bath, but since she would have to put her dirty clothes back on, she decided to wait. She would get cleaned up after she went to the store. She did take the time to wash up a little and make herself presentable. She hoped she looked a little more like a girl now.

As ready as she would ever be to pick out a simple dress for her wedding, she left the hotel room. It wasn't going to be a white gown, but in her heart that didn't matter. What mattered was that Grant loved her—he'd proposed.

Dusty knew Francie was going to be surprised by her wonderful news, and so was Miss Gertrude. The thought of their reactions made her smile as she started from the hotel.

The only store in town was the general store, and Dusty wasn't sure how much clothing would be available there. She thought of the evening she'd spent with Francie when her friend had loaned her the fancy gown and helped style her hair. She wished Francie was with her right then to help her get ready.

The woman behind the counter looked up and smiled when Dusty walked in.

"Afternoon," she said pleasantly.

"Hello." Dusty returned her smile as she came up to the counter. "I need your help."

"Of course, I'll be glad to help you. My name's Kate. What can I get you?"

"I need a dress—to get married in," Dusty explained, and she grinned at the woman's complete look of surprise.

"Oh, my—"

"I know. What I've been wearing lately isn't quite what I planned for my wedding day." Dusty gestured toward the pants, shirt and boots she had on.

"How soon is the wedding?"

"Grant's checking on that with the justice of the peace right now."

Kate came around the counter with a determined look on her face.

"So you don't have much time. Come with me, dear," she said, taking Dusty by the hand to lead her to the back of the store. "I have a few dresses that might work for you."

Half an hour later, Grant stopped by the store to see if Dusty was there, and she spotted him right away. She quickly hung up the dress she was looking at and went to talk to him.

"I spoke with the justice of the peace, and he said he can marry us at five o'clock. That's right before he quits for the day," Grant said.

Dusty knew it was close to four already, so she had just an hour to get ready. "I'll hurry."

"I'll be waiting for you at the hotel," he told her.

Grant made arrangements to pay Kate and then left Dusty to finish her shopping. He returned to the hotel and ordered a bath, taking the time to shave, too. He had a clean shirt and pair of pants with him, and knew they would have to do.

With Kate's help, Dusty picked out a simple day gown that flattered her slender figure, as well as a chemise to wear with it and a pair of shoes to match. Dusty thought about buying a ribbon and trying to fix her hair the way Francie had, but she decided against it. She thought it would take too long to recreate the style, and Grant would be waiting for her.

She hurried back to the hotel and ordered a bath to be brought up. It didn't take long. Once the tub and water were brought to the room, she wasted no time getting undressed and scrubbing herself clean.

Though the heartache of all that had happened was still with her, knowing Grant loved her was enough to get Dusty through these hard times. The thought that he wanted to marry her—tonight— left her almost breathless in anticipation. She knew little about what went on between a man and a woman, but she was sure he was going to teach her all she needed to learn this very night. She smiled, feeling both eager and shy.

After washing her hair, Dusty got out of the tub and dried herself off. It didn't take her long to put on her new clothes, and then she set about trying to make her short hair look feminine. It was one of the few times in her life that she appreciated having a little curl to her hair for the pretty waves covered the mark she still bore from her head wound.

It was only a short time later that Grant knocked on her door. She quickly went to open it and let him in.

Grant stepped into the room and stared at her. His gaze was warm upon her as he took in her demure gown. There was no mistaking Dusty for a boy now. She was a gorgeous woman, and she was going to be his. He went to her and took her in his arms to kiss her.

Dusty responded eagerly to his kiss, looping her arms around his neck and pressing herself against him.

He broke off the kiss and grinned down at her. He wanted her more than he'd ever wanted another woman. "I think we'd better leave for the justice of the peace right now, or we might not make it at all—"

"Oh—" Dusty actually felt herself blushing. "But you know—the thought of staying here and kissing you some more is tempting—"

Grant actually groaned and put some distance between them. "Let's go. When we come back here, I'm not even going to think about leaving this room for the rest of the night."

"Sounds good to me—" she purred. She went to him and drew him down to her for one last kiss. Dusty had never in her life been so bold with a man, but she couldn't resist. "Are you ready?" she asked when they moved apart.

"I'm ready," he answered, and gently took her arm to usher her from the hotel room.

A short time later, Dusty and Grant stood before the justice of the peace and his wife in Mr. Arnold's small office, taking their vows. His wife was serving as their witness.

"Do you, Grant Spencer, take this woman, Justine Martin, to be your lawfully wedded wife?" George Arnold asked as he looked at the Texas Ranger who was standing before him.

"I do," Grant answered solemnly as he looked down at Dusty standing by his side.

The justice of the peace turned to Dusty. "Do you, Justine Martin, take this man, Grant Spencer, to be your lawfully wedded husband?"

"I do," Dusty said, gazing adoringly up at Grant.

"Do you have a ring?" he asked Grant.

"I didn't have time to get one," Grant explained.

"All right, then I now pronounce you man and wife," he pronounced, smiling warmly at them. "You may kiss your bride."

Grant didn't need to be encouraged, but he was respectful as he drew Dusty to him and kissed her chastely.

"Congratulations!" Mrs. Arnold said.

"Thank you." Dusty was smiling brightly as she and Grant started from the office.

They hadn't eaten since their meager breakfast at the campsite, so they stopped at the small restaurant in town for dinner. They ate quickly, hardly able to keep their eyes off each other. It was just sundown as they returned to the hotel.

The clerk saw them come in and did an actual double take when he caught sight of Dusty in her dress. He'd had no idea she was a girl when the two had checked in, but he knew she was one now.

When they reached the hallway, Dusty stopped Grant in front of her room.

"Let's stay in my room tonight—" She slowly unlocked and opened the door, then turned to look up at him, a tempting look in her eyes. "When you found me in here the last time, you were expecting trouble— What are you expecting tonight?"

Heat flared in Grant's regard and he swept her up into his arms to carry her across the threshold. "From you? Still trouble—and lots of it."

His voice was low and sexy and sent a shiver of sensual awareness through Dusty. She linked her arms around his neck and pulled him to her for a hungry kiss.

Grant kicked the door shut without ending the kiss. He didn't want to break it off, but he had to in order to lock the door and draw the shade so there would be no interruptions.

He turned back to find Dusty just standing there watching him. She looked a little bit lost, and he smiled tenderly as he went to her and drew her close.

"You are a beautiful woman, Mrs. Spencer," he said, claiming her lips in a hungry kiss.

Just hearing him call her "Mrs. Spencer" sent a thrill through Dusty. She returned his kiss, wanting him as she'd never wanted any man before.

Instinctively, she needed to be close to him.

She needed to be one with him.

Dusty didn't feel any shyness when Grant began to work at the buttons on her dress.

Grant managed to free her quickly from the garment and then looked down at her as she stood before him clad only in her chemise. He smiled again as he lifted her in his arms and carried her to the bed. He laid Dusty there and stepped back to strip off his shirt and boots. He thought about taking off the rest of his clothes, but hesitated. He knew she was an innocent and he didn't want to do anything to make her uncomfortable right now. He wanted this night to be perfect for them. Joining her on the bed, he moved over her and kissed her.

Dusty was on fire. Passion unlike anything she'd ever known burned within her and she held Grant close, thrilling at the touch of his bare, hard-muscled chest against her. She caressed his back and shoulders and shivered and arched against him in love's age-old invitation as his lips left hers to trace a heated path of kisses down the side of her neck.

"I love you, Dusty," Grant whispered as he rose up over her.

She smiled up at him, an innocent yet seductive smile. "I love you, too."

With infinite tenderness, he helped her slip out of her chemise and then left her side just long enough to shed the rest of his clothes. There were no barriers between them as he returned to their marriage bed. With gentle yet arousing caresses, he ignited the flames of her desire, and they came together in a surge of excitement that left them both breathless with its splendor.

Grant was careful as he taught her love's ways, showing her how to move with him and making her fully his own. When ecstasy claimed them, they collapsed together, holding each other tightly as they cherished the beauty they had just shared.

"I never knew—" Dusty whispered to him, pressing a soft kiss to his shoulder as she lay against him.

He cradled her to him, never wanting to let her go. He realized as she slowly ran her hand over his chest that she had no idea just how seductive her actions were. He pulled her beneath him and met her in a hungry, devouring kiss.

Dusty surrendered to the magic of his loving, cherishing each moment that they had together, and knowing she never wanted to be apart from him again.

It was much later in the night that an exhausted Dusty lay sound asleep in Grant's arms. He looked down at her as she slept, and was certain he'd never known another woman like her. She was amazing, and he wondered now what the future held for them. As a Ranger he would be moving around a lot, and his wife couldn't travel with him. That troubled him. He didn't want to leave her alone for extended lengths of time. He wanted to know she was safe and protected. And he wanted her with him.

For a moment he considered leaving the Rangers, but he knew he couldn't quit right now. First, he had to find out what had happened to Frank. He planned to ride out with Dusty in the morning and search for the answer to his friend's disappearance.

Grant closed his eyes to rest, treasuring the memory of the loving he and Dusty had just shared.

Chapter Twenty-five

It was before dawn when Dusty slowly awoke to find herself nestled against Grant's side, her head resting on his shoulder. He was still asleep, so she took the time to just watch him, loving this moment of complete privacy.

He loved her—

They were married—

A part of her still couldn't believe that her whole life had changed so quickly. One moment she'd thought she was looking into the abyss of what her future was going to be without her father, and now, she was married to the man she loved.

Her gaze went over him. Relaxed in a deep sleep, his tanned, ruggedly handsome features were less hardened, and he looked younger. She honestly believed he was the most handsome man she'd ever seen. Her gaze swept lower across the broad width of his powerful chest and arms, and she remembered just how wonderful it felt to be held in those arms, cradled against his chest.

Dusty found herself wondering more about him. She realized she knew very little about

Grant's past or his family. She didn't even know why he had decided to become a lawman. The mystery intrigued her and she was determined to find out about his past.

She lifted her gaze to find he had woken and was watching her with a heated glint in his eyes.

"You're awake—" she said in a soft, husky voice as she rose up on her elbow and leaned down to kiss him.

When the kissed ended, he smiled at her.

"If I wasn't before, I am now," he growled seductively as he brought her beneath him.

"Good—"

Grant needed no more encouragement.

They made love quickly, each kiss and caress arousing them to new heights as they strove for the fulfillment of being one again. When at last they reached the pinnacle of their passion, they lay together, glorying in the aftermath of their love.

When they'd both caught their breath, Grant knew he and Dusty had to decide what she was going to do while he went in search of Frank.

"You know that as soon as I hear back from my captain, I'm going to ride for Eagle Ridge—" he began.

Dusty was all but holding her breath as she waited to hear what he was going to say next. Her heart was aching at the thought that he might tell her she had to return to Canyon Springs by herself and wait for him there. She didn't speak, but waited in silence for him to go on.

"And I want you to ride with me," he finished.

"You do?" Her spirits lifted at his words.

"Yes, love. I want you along," Grant said seriously. He saw the tears in her eyes and didn't understand why she was crying. "What's wrong?"

"Nothing," Dusty managed in a choked voice as she leaned close to kiss him. "I was afraid you were going to send me back to Canyon Springs on a stage and then you were going to ride off by yourself to try to find your friend. I want to go with you. I want to help you while you're doing this. I am your partner, you know."

"In more ways than one," he said as he kissed her.

Nearly an hour passed before they finally got out of bed.

"When will we be leaving?" Dusty asked as she watched him get dressed.

"As soon as I get a wire back from my captain," Grant answered, smiling as he looked over to find her still sitting on the side of the bed with the sheet wrapped demurely around her. He was more than tempted to make love to her again, but he knew if he got her back in bed, they might not leave the room all day. The promise of being locked in the privacy of the hotel room with Dusty was exciting, but he knew it was important they ride for Eagle Ridge. The sooner he got there, the better. "Why?"

"Well, I was wondering if you wanted Justine to go to breakfast with you or Dusty?" she asked with a grin.

"This morning, I definitely want my bride to have breakfast with me—and it doesn't matter to me what she wears, although I have to admit I do like what she's wearing right now."

Dusty was laughing as he came to stand before her and gave her one last quick kiss.

"Turn your back while I get dressed," she said, feeling suddenly a little shy now that it was daylight.

Grant chuckled and did as he was told. Although he did appreciate catching sight of her reflection in the mirror as she put on her dress again.

They went to the restaurant to get breakfast, and it was there the clerk from the telegraph office found them.

"I figured you hadn't left town yet, Ranger Spencer," the clerk said as he gave Grant the message from his captain and the money he'd been wired.

"No, I was waiting to hear from you," Grant told him. "Thanks."

Grant quickly read his captain's short message.

"What did he say?" Dusty asked.

"He was glad to hear about Jackson and the gang," Grant began, and then his mood grew more solemn, "and he said he hadn't heard from Frank at all. That I should go see what I could find out in Eagle Ridge."

"Good. How soon are we riding out?"

The serious Grant she was used to dealing with was back as he looked across the table at her.

"Right after we eat and get the supplies we need."

"I'll be ready when you are," she promised.

They quickly finished their meal and went back

to the general store. This time Dusty got herself a new pair of pants and another shirt, along with food and ammunition they would need for the trip. They returned to the hotel to pack up.

Knowing it would be quite a while before they had the chance to share a comfortable bed again, Dusty didn't hesitate to take advantage of this—their last moment alone in the hotel room.

"Could you help me out of my dress?" she asked.

Considering how modest she'd been earlier, Grant was surprised by her request, but he wasn't about to turn her down. As he came to unfasten the buttons for her, she quickly reached up and kissed him.

"I thought you needed help with your dress," he said with a slight smile.

"I do," she said a bit breathlessly, "and it seems like you're moving awful slow this morning."

Grant quickly proved her wrong.

It was an hour later when they rode out of Gold Canyon.

It would take at least four days of hard riding to get to Eagle Ridge, so they didn't waste any time. They maintained a steady pace and rode until sundown before stopping to make camp for the night. With the morning light, they were on their way again.

It was late that afternoon when a storm came through, and they had to stop and find some shelter under a rocky outcropping to wait out the downpour. Dusty huddled near Grant as the storm raged across the land.

"I've been wondering—" she began. "When did you decide you wanted to become a lawman?"

"My father was a sheriff, so I'd thought about it growing up, but I guess I was fifteen when I made the final decision."

"Why then?"

Grant looked over at her as he told her the story of that fateful day when his father had been gunned down. "The Gradys took me in, and I stayed with them until I was old enough to become a Ranger. It's what I've been doing ever since."

Dusty put a hand on his arm. "I'm sorry about your father."

"So am I. He was a good man. He didn't deserve what happened to him."

"I understand." Her heart was heavy as she thought of her own father.

Their gazes met.

"I know you do," he sympathized.

"I'm sure your father would be proud of you," Dusty said.

"I hope so. I've always tried to do my best."

They fell silent again as they waited for the weather to clear.

Almost an hour passed before they could ride out again, but when they stopped for the night, they were glad to find the nearby creek had water.

After two days of travel in the heat, the creek looked very inviting to Dusty. Grant was busy building the campfire, so she went down to the water's edge to look around. The water looked tempting, and since there was a little sunlight left, she quickly took

off her boots and socks and rolled up her pants' legs
to go wading. The water felt wonderful. When Grant
came to see what she was doing, she couldn't help
herself. She bent down and splashed him.

"Are you looking for trouble, woman?" he asked.

"Why? Have I found it?" she laughed, deliberately splashing him again.

"Oh, yeah." Grant paused only long enough to
toss his gun belt aside, and then he went in after
her.

Dusty squealed in delight at his pursuit. She
tried to escape, but he was too fast for her. He
grabbed her up and dropped her in the water, soak-
ing her thoroughly. She came up drenched, but
laughing.

"Join me—" she invited.

She was more than a little disappointed when he
walked out of the water, but her disappointment
didn't last long. In one smooth movement, he
pulled off his shirt. She joined him on the bank,
and they quickly shed their clothes and ran back
into the water to enjoy the moment.

With the waist-deep water swirling about them,
Grant held her close to kiss her. Dusty responded
fully, thrilled to be in his arms. Desire flooded
through them, and Grant knew he had to have her.
He carried her back up to the campsite and laid
her on his bedroll. They came together in a rush,
their passion driving them on.

Later, their desire sated, Grant smiled into the
darkness as he murmured, "I like going swimming
with you."

"I like swimming with you, too. I think we'll have to do it more often," Dusty teased.

At peace, they slept through the night and were again up and ready to ride early the next morning. They still had a long way to go.

Chapter Twenty-six

It was late in the morning and Andy was working in the stable when he heard a rider coming in. He took a quick look outside and spotted his father approaching the ranch. Disgust filled him. Lately, his pa had been spending more days—and nights—in town, and Andy was more than a little scared. He hurried back into the stable and went back to work. He wanted to avoid talking to his father as much as he could. After spending the entire night in town, Andy knew his father's mood was going to be ugly, and when he was in a bad mood, he got mean.

Nat had just spent the night drinking and gambling—and losing—and then drinking some more. The other gamblers' smug arrogance as they'd raked in their winnings at the poker table had left him furious, and his anger hadn't lessened on the ride home.

Nat rode straight to the stable and dismounted to look around. When he spotted Andy inside, he stalked into the stable to confront him.

"What the hell you doing in here?" Nat demanded.

"Cleaning out the stalls, Pa," Andy answered. He didn't dare look up, so he just kept shoveling.

"You look at me when I talk to you!" Nat snarled, storming over to Andy and grabbing him by the arm to forcefully spin him around.

"Yes, Pa," Andy answered. He could smell the liquor on his father, and he feared what was coming next.

"What have you been doing since yesterday? It don't look like you've cleaned much of anything! This stable is filthy!"

Without any warning, he backhanded Andy, knocking him backward to the ground and bloodying his lip.

"Pa—don't!" Andy cried out as his father came after him again.

Sarah had been doing the laundry out behind the house when she thought she heard Andy yelling. She dropped what she was doing and hurried around the house to see what was wrong. As soon as she'd spotted her father's horse in front of the stable, she knew there was trouble. She raced inside to get her iron skillet and came running back out to help her brother.

"You're gonna learn how to earn your keep, you lazy little—" Nat was letting his anger rule as he pulled off his belt and got ready to lash Andy mercilessly.

Andy was cowering before him. He'd tried to run out of the stable, but his father had chased him down and thrown him to the ground again.

"Pa! Don't! Leave Andy alone!" Sarah yelled as

she came racing into the barn to find him abusing her little brother.

Nat paused for a moment and glared at her, ready to beat her next. "You don't tell me what to do, you little—"

"Don't hurt Andy, Pa— You're drunk. Just go inside and leave us alone," she ordered, holding the iron skillet like a weapon.

"You're just like your ma—always trying to tell me what to do! I run this ranch!" Nat was all but screaming now. "You get out of here!"

"No! I'm not leaving Andy!"

Andy scrambled to his feet and tried to flee, but Nat was too fast for him. He grabbed his son by the arm and threw him back into the stall, then turned to start beating him again.

"Pa—stop it—" Sarah was sobbing as she ran forward to save her brother. She hit her father on the back with the skillet. She'd hoped to hit him on the head and knock him out, but she'd missed, and now she knew she was in even bigger trouble.

"Why—you—" Nat turned on her and slapped her, then began to beat her, too.

"No— Pa! Stop—" Andy was hitting his father with what little power he had, trying to help his sister.

Just then, two strong hands grabbed Nat and pulled him bodily away from Sarah.

"Get away from her, you drunk!" Frank ordered as he threw the older man halfway across the stable.

Nat landed against one of the support posts and then fell heavily. He lay in a daze, staring around himself.

"Ranger—" Sarah looked up to see him coming to her aid.

Frank knelt down on one knee beside her to check her injuries. "Are you all right? Where did he hit you?"

"Sarah—" Andy ran into the stall to be with her.

Frank glanced at the boy and saw that he was bleeding. "You all right, boy?"

"I think so. Just a little blood, that's all—" Andy answered in a manly way.

Frank was proud of Andy and the fact that he was more concerned about his sister's injuries than his own. "Let's see how she is—"

While they were checking on Sarah, Nat got to his feet, furious at the way the stranger had interfered in his family's business. He saw the iron skillet that Sarah had dropped and he picked it up, ready for revenge. He was unsteady on his feet, but he staggered over to the stall.

"Ranger! Look out!" Andy hollered when he caught sight of his father coming toward them.

Frank had just started to turn when Nat hit him. It was a glancing blow on the side of his head and the Ranger fell back against the side of the stall. Half sitting, half lying down, Frank was dazed by the force of the blow. He stared around himself in confusion, his head throbbing as he tried to figure out where he was and what had happened.

"Pa! Stop it!"

Andy jumped on his father's back to distract him from beating Sarah, and Nat yanked the boy off him, then hit him with his fist.

When Frank saw Nat hit Andy, he frowned.

And he remembered—

His life returned to him.

Frank remembered chasing the Jackson gang—

He remembered the ambush—

Jackson and his gunmen!

Where were they?

Were they hiding out somewhere near the ranch?

Frank knew immediately he had to go after the killers—

They were out there somewhere—

All the memories of his past returned, too, including the way his father had beaten him as a young boy—just like Nat was beating Andy.

Frank gave a shake of his head at the sight before him, and immediately got up to go after the drunken fool. He would see that Andy and Sarah were safe and then he would get Jackson.

Frank charged over and took Nat by the shoulder. He forcefully spun the drunk around and hit him in the jaw with all his might, knocking him down.

Nat lay on the ground groaning and crying like a baby.

"What's the matter, you old drunk? You only like fighting women and boys?" he challenged..

In a fury, Nat got up and went after the Ranger, but he was no match for Frank. He could beat up children and girls, but not a full-grown man. Frank handled him easily, and the old drunk finally collapsed, unconscious on the stable floor.

Frank looked over at Sarah, who was sitting huddled in the stall, holding Andy in her arms. He was thankful that her old man hadn't beaten her too severely. She'd have some bruises, but she'd recover. He knew then what a lucky boy Andy was, to have a sister like Sarah.

Frank's mood was determined as he went to the brother and sister and helped them up. He kept his arms around them supportively as they moved past their unconscious father.

"Move quick now. Get up to the house and pack your things," he ordered.

"What?" Sarah looked up at him, confused by this sudden change in his manner. He was confident and commanding. A man completely sure of himself.

Frank looked down at her and saw the woman he wanted to spend the rest of his life with. "The only good thing about this fight was that I got my memory back. My name is Frank Thomas, and I rode out here after the Jackson gang."

"Les Jackson?" Sarah asked, nervously.

"That's the one."

"They're the ones who ambushed you? I had no idea they were in the area," she said in a shocked tone.

"Since they haven't come looking for me, I've got a feeling they rode on. I'm going after them, but first I'm getting both you and your brother out of here—now. We're leaving."

"Leaving?" Andy looked frightened.

"That's right. I plan on marrying your sister if she'll have me, and you're coming with us."

Sarah gasped at his shocking proposal. "You want to marry me?"

"I love you, Sarah," he told her quickly. "And now that I've got my memory back, I know I don't have a wife and family waiting for me anywhere. I want you and Andy to be my family. Will you marry me?"

"Yes—yes, oh, yes!" She hugged him fiercely, unable to believe all that had happened so fast.

"Go pack. I'm going to get one of the ranch hands out here to keep an eye on your father."

Sarah didn't even look at her father as she grabbed Andy's hand and they rushed from the stable.

Frank took a look at Nat and knew he wasn't seriously injured. He went and found Chet and told him his plans.

Chet looked at Frank with admiration. "You're a fine man, Ranger Thomas," he said, smiling as he used the Ranger's real name for the first time.

"I'm thankful for all your help. Just don't let the old fool come after us. I want to get Sarah and Andy away from here. They don't deserve what he's been doing to them."

"I know," Chet said, regretfully. He stepped forward to shake Frank's hand, glad that he was back to being his normal self.

"Warn Nat not to come after us."

"I will," the ranch hand promised. "I'll have the horses saddled up and ready for you shortly."

"I appreciate it." Frank nodded and left Chet

there to tend to Nat and get their horses ready while he went up to the house. He knew he would owe Nat some money for the horse when this was all over, but he'd worry about that later. Right now, he had to see that Sarah and Andy were taken care of, and then he had to go after Jackson and contact Grant.

Sarah was standing in the parlor with a small traveling bag, looking a bit lost when Frank let himself in.

"Are you ready?" Frank asked, coming to her side.

Sarah turned quickly to him and went into his arms. She was still terrified from the beating her father had given her. She had no idea what would have happened to her and Andy if her Ranger hadn't shown up to save them when he did. "I think so—"

Andy came running in to join them then. He had one bag with him and he was carrying a rifle, too. "Let's get out of here—Frank," he said, using his name for the first time.

Frank smiled down at Andy and, keeping an arm around Sarah, he hugged the boy to him with his other arm. "Let's ride."

"Here. You may need this, Frank," Andy said, looking up at him with pure admiration in his eyes as he handed him the rifle.

"I appreciate it, Andy." He took the rifle and checked it over.

As they started from the house, Sarah looked

back once more, knowing they would never return to this place that had been their home.

Chet was bringing their horses up as the three of them came to stand outside.

"Is he stirring yet?" Frank asked. He was ready for more trouble if the old man wanted to give it to him.

"Yeah, but I told him to stay down at the stable."

Frank looked that way and was glad to see no sign of the old fool. He didn't want to have to fight Sarah's father again.

"Thanks, Chet," Sarah and Andy told him as they tied their bags on the backs of their saddles and mounted up.

Frank swung himself onto his horse and led the way from the ranch house, all the while keeping an eye on the stable doorway. He wouldn't put it past Nat to try something crazy. Once they'd ridden out of sight of the stable, Frank was finally satisfied he could relax.

"So you really got your memory back?" Andy looked over at Frank, his expression wide-eyed and curious.

"That's right, and I'm glad I did. Now, I know exactly what I have to do."

"What's that?" Sarah asked, speaking for the first time since they'd ridden out.

"I have to find a minister in town so we can get married."

"Oh—" She was breathless at the thought.

"Andy, I do have your permission to marry her, don't I?" Frank asked, smiling at the boy.

Andy grinned at him. "Yes, you do. I think it's a fine idea, don't you, Sarah?"

"Oh, yes," Sarah said, tears of joy burning in her eyes as she looked at her Ranger and her brother.

Chapter Twenty-seven

Frank forced himself to get serious again as they rode in closer to Eagle Ridge. He was excited about marrying Sarah and starting a new life with her and Andy, but he also knew Les Jackson was still out there somewhere. True, no one had heard anything about the gang being in town, but that didn't mean the outlaws weren't still in the area.

Frank was glad he still had his gun, and he was even gladder that Andy had thought to bring along the rifle. He was ready for whatever trouble might come his way, whether from Nat or the Jackson gang.

He looked over at Sarah as she rode next him. "Let's go to the hotel first, and then we can pay your reverend a visit. Do you have any friends in town? Anyone you'd like to come to the wedding?" In the weeks that he'd been on the ranch, she'd never visited with any friends, but he thought she might have someone in town she was close to.

"Not really. We seldom went into town except to get supplies or to go to church every once in a while. Mostly, Pa wanted us to stay on the ranch."

When Frank heard what a controlling man Nat was, he was even more grateful that he'd gotten Sarah and Andy away from him.

"You don't mind that it will be just us?"

"No," she said sincerely. Her dream was coming true, and she couldn't have been happier.

Before long, they had taken rooms at the hotel and were at the church, talking with Reverend Crawford in his small office.

Reverend Crawford's expression was concerned as he looked at Sarah. "Are you certain you don't want your father here for the ceremony?"

Sarah looked up at the preacher and met his regard straight on. "I'm certain, Reverend Crawford."

Andy understood how hurt his sister was, and he wanted the preacher to know exactly how they felt about their old man.

"He ain't coming anywhere near my sister ever again," Andy asserted. Real men didn't abuse their loved ones like their father, real men defended and protected them. He'd learned that from Frank.

"I see," the reverend responded. He'd heard the talk around town about why Sarah and Andy's mother had run away some years ago, but that had happened before he had come to Eagle Ridge. He could understand why Sarah and her brother wanted no part of their father. "And you want the ceremony to take place today?"

"Yes, if you can arrange it," Frank said. He looked over at Sarah to find she was smiling at him.

Reverend Crawford had married eloping couples

before, so their request wasn't too surprising. "Let's plan on this evening. Be here at the church at seven."

Frank stood up and shook hands with the preacher. "We'll be here."

They left the church office and went outside. Frank took a look around. He saw no signs of Nat or any of the Jackson gang.

"I'm going to wire my captain and let him know what happened. Maybe he's heard something from Grant about the gang."

"What will you do if they are still on the loose?" Sarah asked worriedly.

"We'll worry about that when the time comes." Even as he said it, Frank knew if Grant hadn't brought in the outlaws, he would have to. Before he rode out, though, he would make sure Sarah and Andy were safe. "Andy, why don't you go with Sarah back to the hotel? I'll be along in a little while."

"I want to go with you, Frank," Andy said without hesitation.

Frank was surprised, but didn't mind the boy's company. "All right. Let's get over to the telegraph office."

They walked on and once he saw Sarah go into the hotel, Andy stopped and drew Frank off to the side of a building.

"Here—" he said, reaching deep in his pocket and pulling out a small plain gold band that was obviously worn. He handed it to Frank.

"What's this?"

"You're going to need it for the wedding. It belonged to my grandmother. After you said you were going to marry Sarah, I brought it along 'cause I figured you wouldn't have one."

Frank looked down at Andy, deeply touched by what he'd done. "You're a fine young man, Andy."

The boy grinned up at him, knowing such praise from Frank was a great honor, indeed.

They went on to send the wire and returned to the hotel.

"We gonna get to eat anytime soon? I got the money for it," Andy said. As a growing boy, he was always thinking about food.

Frank was looking forward to hearing back from his captain so he would have some money again. It didn't sit well with him, being so dependent on others, but right then he didn't have a choice. "Why don't you run up and get your sister? We've got enough time to have some dinner right now."

Andy was glad he'd brought it up, and they were soon eating a hearty meal at the local restaurant. It was nearly six o'clock when they returned to get ready for the wedding.

Andy and Sarah were in the room they were sharing for the time being, getting dressed. Sarah was standing before the mirror, checking to make sure she looked her best.

"You love him, don't you?" Andy asked her cautiously, just wanting to make sure she was making the right decision.

Sarah turned to her little brother. "I loved him even before I knew who he really was, but I was always afraid that he might have a family already—a family who was out there somewhere, missing him and worrying about him. Finding out that he doesn't is a dream come true for me."

"And now he's going to have that family. He's going to have us," Andy said, smiling happily at the realization that they would never be threatened by their father again.

"And we're going to have him," she added.

Sarah had packed only one dress when she'd left the house that morning. She wore it now, ready for what she knew was going to be the most important moment in her life—her marriage to Frank.

Andy put on his change of clothes and was waiting for his sister when the knock came at the door. He hurried to let Frank in.

"It's about time to go over to church," Frank said, eager to be on their way. He had been alone for a long time, but after tonight he would never be alone again.

"We're ready," Sarah assured him.

"I was wondering if you'd back out on me," he teased.

"Never," she told him, giving him a quick, chaste kiss. "Let's go."

"Yeah," Andy added, "you gotta marry my sister."

Reverend Crawford and another man were waiting for them by the church's front doors. Sarah recognized the second man as Paul Wagner, a deacon with the church, whom she had met a few times over the years.

"Sarah, it's so good to see you," Paul greeted. "Reverend Crawford asked if I could serve as the witness to your marriage, and I was honored."

"Thank you, Mr. Wagner."

Sarah introduced him to Frank.

"Are you ready?" Reverend Crawford asked.

Frank looked down at Sarah. "I am."

"So am I," she said with a tender smile.

"Andy, would you like to escort your sister up the aisle?" The reverend looked at the boy expectantly.

Andy's eyes widened. "Oh, yes."

"All right. Give us a moment to get ready. When the music starts, you can bring her to the altar."

Andy nodded, his expression completely serious as he focused on the serious task ahead.

"You've got music for us?" Sarah was surprised.

"I thought it would be appropriate," the reverend answered. "My wife was happy to oblige."

Reverend Crawford led the way to the front of the church with Frank and Paul following behind. He instructed them where to stand and then nodded to his wife, who began to play the small organ nearby.

Sarah looked up toward the front of the church, loving the sight of Frank standing there looking so tall and handsome. He was watching her as tenderly as she was watching him, and she knew she loved him with all her heart. She couldn't believe that in just minutes he would be hers forever. She offered up a prayer of thanks to God that she and Andy had found him when he'd been shot.

She didn't even want to think about what might have happened to Frank if they hadn't come upon him that day.

Andy heard the music and looked nervously up at Sarah, whispering, "I guess it's time—"

She was smiling serenely as the music swelled around her, sending a shiver of excitement through her. "I'm ready."

The reverend nodded to Andy to bring her forward, and Sarah took her brother's arm and started up the aisle of the church with him.

Frank watched her make her way up the aisle with Andy and thought he'd never seen a more beautiful bride. He knew how blessed he'd been that Sarah and Andy had come into his life, and he intended to spend the rest of his days showing them just how much he loved them.

Andy stopped beside Frank and handed Sarah over to him. Then he went to stand with Paul and watch the ceremony.

The music stopped and Reverend Crawford began the wedding. It didn't take him long to marry them.

Sarah almost felt like she was dreaming as he announced that Frank and she were now man and wife.

"You may kiss your bride," Reverend Crawford told Frank.

Frank didn't say a word. He just took Sarah in his arms and gave her a big kiss. Long moments later, they broke apart and were congratulated by the preacher, his wife and their witness.

Andy was standing there, beaming up at the two of them. He looked at his sister, all the love he had for her shining in his eyes as he said, "I brought the ring for you."

Sarah kissed him tenderly on the cheek as she said with heartfelt tenderness, "I know."

Andy was touched by the love in her expression, and he quickly turned to Frank to gather himself. "Looks like you're stuck with her now, Frank."

"I think I'm up to handling her. What do you think?" Frank returned.

"I know you are."

They left the church, a true family in the eyes of God.

Much later that night, when they were certain Andy was asleep in his room, Sarah and Frank were finally alone together.

Frank embraced her and kissed her hungrily, letting her know how much he wanted and needed her. Sarah was excited by his kiss, yet she also felt a bit unsure of herself and drew back a little.

Frank glanced down at her, wondering why she was pulling away from him. "What is it, Sarah?"

She actually blushed as she told him, "Frank— I—"

He had no idea what she was about to say.

"Is something wrong?" he pressed.

"No, it's just that—" Sarah looked a bit lost. "I don't know what I should do."

He gave a deep, sensuous chuckle as he pulled her back tightly against him. "Were you good in school?"

Sarah frowned, having no idea what his question had to do with their wedding night. "Yes, I was a good student."

"Good, because I'm going to teach you everything you need to know—right now. Are you ready for your first lesson?"

She smiled up at him enticingly. "Will there be homework?"

"Every night," he growled, lifting her in his arms to carry her to the bed for her first lesson in loving.

Later, as he held her close, he had to admit she was a very good student and a very fast learner.

They were still sound asleep the next morning when Andy came pounding on the door. "It's late! Aren't you hungry? I'm ready for breakfast!"

Sarah and Frank awoke with a start, having gotten very little sleep the night before.

"Give us a few minutes and we'll be ready."

"I'll be in my room," Andy called through the locked door.

Frank looked over at her and kissed her quickly. "I'd love to spend the whole day here with you, but I think Andy might get a little mad at me."

"He'd be mad at both of us, because I don't want to get up either," she purred, holding him close for a moment before releasing him and getting up. "Andy's not a patient boy."

"I can tell," Frank chuckled.

A short time later, as they were leaving the hotel on their way to the restaurant, the clerk from the telegraph office saw them passing by and called to Frank.

"Your wire just came in," the clerk told Frank.

They went into the office and the clerk handed him the money that had been wired to him, along with the message from his captain.

"You're going to want to read that right away. You got some good news there, Ranger Thomas," the clerk said.

Frank quickly read the message and started to smile.

"What is it?" Sarah asked.

"The captain was shocked to hear from me. Grant wired him earlier this week with the news that the Jackson gang had told him I was dead."

"So your friend caught the gang?" Andy asked.

"Yes, Grant did it— Two of them are dead, and the other two are locked up. They won't be hurting anyone again."

"Your friend must be a fine Ranger," the boy said, impressed.

"That's right, and he's on his way here to Eagle Ridge right now to look for me. He should be showing up any day."

Sarah hugged her new husband. "I'm so glad your friend brought them in. That means you don't have to ride after the outlaws again."

Frank's expression darkened a bit. "I would have liked to have been there, just to see the looks on their faces when they found out I was still alive, but that's all right. Their days of robbing and killing are over. That's all that matters."

"What are you going to do now?"

"I'm taking you home. I've got a small spread near Dry Springs."

"Are you going to keep working as a Ranger?" Andy asked.

"Yes. There will be times when I have to ride out. There's always going to be trouble, and it's my job to take care of it."

Sarah hadn't known Frank had a ranch. "We've got a home?"

Frank gave her a tender look. "Yes, we do."

Just then he heard a shout.

"Frank?"

Frank turned quickly to see Grant riding down the street. Frank waved and stepped out into the street to greet his friend as Grant galloped up with what appeared to be a teenage boy following close behind him.

"I think your friend is here," Andy said with a big grin.

Grant reined in and quickly dismounted to stand beside his friend. He couldn't believe his eyes. He hadn't allowed himself to hope too much that he'd find Frank alive. "I can't believe it— They told me you were dead—"

"I know. I just got a wire from the captain this morning, telling me you brought the gang in. Good job."

Frank shook hands with Grant, and they shared a look of true understanding. Grant could see that Frank had a new scar from a recent head wound.

"I'm glad you came to find me," Frank said. "I've got a lot to tell you."

"I've got a lot to tell you, too," Grant countered. Looking back to Dusty, he called out, "Dusty, I just found out Frank's alive and well."

"I had that feeling," Dusty said happily as she dismounted to stand beside him.

"You're a girl—" Frank said in surprise.

"I get that reaction a lot," she laughed.

"Frank, this is Dusty, my wife."

Frank was shocked by the news, and his smile broadened. "Congratulations— I've got someone I want you to meet, too." He looked over at Sarah and Andy, and they came to join him. "Sarah, Andy, this is Grant Spencer and his wife, Dusty. Grant, this is my wife, Sarah, and my brother-in-law, Andy."

Grant was equally surprised by Frank's news. "I think we've got a lot of catching up to do."

"I know we do," Frank agreed.

"We were just going to eat breakfast," Andy said, looking from Grant to Dusty. "You want to come with us?"

"That sounds great," Grant replied.

He and Dusty tied up their horses, and they all moved off down the street.

"So what happened to you?" Grant asked.

Frank slanted him a sidelong grin as he began. "It's a long story. The good news is I can remember it all now."

Epilogue

Six Months Later
Canyon Springs

Music filled the church as Fred escorted Francie down the aisle.

Everyone was watching as she passed by. She was the epitome of the beautiful bride in her white gown and veil.

Fred stopped before the altar and handed his daughter over to his future son-in-law before going to sit with his wife.

Rick took her hand and smiled down at her. Francie was a bit teary-eyed as she watched her father walk away to join her mother in a pew, but then she turned back to Rick and her spirits soared.

This was the day she'd waited for all her life.

She was finally going to be married to Rick!

Excitement filled her as the minister began the wedding ceremony.

Dusty was sitting with Grant and Miss Gertrude in a pew near the front. She was thrilled for Francie, and hoped her marriage to Rick would turn out to be as wonderful as her own marriage to Grant. She had truly found her partner in him.

When Grant realized she was watching him, he

gave her a questioning look, but she just smiled at him. She glanced down at the new wedding ring she was wearing before turning back to watch Francie and Rick take their vows.

When the ceremony had ended and Francie and Rick had moved back down the aisle to leave the church, Miss Gertrude stood with Dusty and Grant to follow them out.

"It's such a shame you two didn't get to have a big wedding like this," she told them.

Grant slipped an arm around Dusty and drew her close. "You're right, Miss Gertrude, but the important thing is that I didn't let her get away from me."

Dusty was laughing. Her married life with Grant was a dream come true for her.

The old lady went to Grant and pulled him down to kiss him on the cheek.

"You are a fine man, Sheriff Spencer." Miss Gertrude had been delighted when the town got rid of the old sheriff and Grant decided to leave the Rangers and run for the job. He'd been elected easily and was doing a wonderful job of keeping Canyon Springs safe.

"Thank you, Miss Gertrude." He'd come to care deeply for the elderly woman. He'd liked her since the first time he'd met her at the town dance, and he'd learned now what a wonderful influence she'd been on Dusty.

As they started filing from the church, Miss Gertrude moved on ahead of them. Grant caught Dusty by the arm and held her back for a moment alone.

"You're not sorry we got married so quickly, are you?" he asked.

Dusty looked up at the man she loved and drew him down to her to give him a tender kiss. "All that matters is that we're together. We're partners, remember?" she teased.

"You're right." Grant smiled at her, knowing "the kid" was the best partner he'd ever had.

"I love you, Grant."

"I love you, too, Dusty."

INTERACT WITH DORCHESTER ONLINE!

Want to learn more about your favorite books and authors?
Want to talk with other readers that like to read the same books as you?
Want to see up-to-the-minute Dorchester news?

VISIT DORCHESTER AT:

DorchesterPub.com
Twitter.com/DorchesterPub
Facebook.com (Search Pages)

DISCUSS DORCHESTER'S NOVELS AT:

Dorchester Forums at DorchesterPub.com
GoodReads.com
LibraryThing.com
Myspace.com/books
Shelfari.com
WeRead.com

Dawn McTavish

A HARD MAN

Trace Ord was a renegade rider, a wrangler sent to round up horses that strayed or were rustled from their owners. He was born to the saddle and could shoot the wings off a bee in flight, and he'd seen his share of action. A man like himself couldn't live past thirty in post–Civil War Arizona and not come up against some bandit or cardsharp itching to throw lead.

A HARDER SITUATION

His current job had Trace working for two ranchers up north who were certain he'd find their stock at the Lazy C. Getting those horses back would be anything but easy. The owner of the Lazy C was as mean as any hombre living, and he and his men were more than willing to trade bullets. His wife was a touch more dangerous. The desperate beauty found Trace on the plains . . . and she stole both his prize stallion and his heart.

Renegade Riders

ISBN 13: 978-0-8439-6322-9

Constance O'Banyon

The Vision

He'd been named Wind Warrior and called the savior of
his Blackfoot people. But the mystical power that filled
him awoke his bother's hatred and envy. Dull Knife
would do anything to take what was his.

The Woman

Slender and lovely, the white captive had long ago
caught Wind Warrior's eye. She was the kind of beauty
that could make a man forget all else in the exquisite
pleasures of the night. But when Dull Knife plotted to
steal her away, the rivalry between the two brothers
would come to a head, a prophecy would be fulfilled
and with her daring rescue, a great passion would be
born.

Wind Warrior

ISBN 13: 978-0-8439-6301-4

LISA COOKE

"Mega fun, fast-paced and with a sexy to-die-for hero—
my favorite kind of historical romance."
—Lori Foster on *Texas Hold Him*

A Midwife Crisis

THREE MEN AND A LADY

Katie's family has decided she needs a husband. And
when Katie's family puts their mind to something, it's as
good as done. In fact, they're so good, they've arranged
three fiancés for her in less than a week! What's a midwife
to do? Katie figures the best course is exactly what she
tells her patients: bear down and push through it.

Dr. John Keffer is used to helping people. It's why he
came back to the Appalachian Mountains—to build a
new practice and leave behind painful memories in the
big city. But usually his help is of a medical nature, not
advising the most captivating woman he's ever met which
man to wed. Especially when he's not even on the short
list. With a good dose of wooing, he hopes to convince
Katie that marrying *him* is just what the doctor ordered.

ISBN 13: 978-0-8439-6362-5

☐ **YES!**

Sign me up for the Historical Romance Book Club and send my FREE BOOKS! If I choose to stay in the club, I will pay only $8.50* each month, a savings of $6.48!

NAME: _____

ADDRESS: _____

TELEPHONE: _____

EMAIL: _____

☐ I want to pay by credit card.

☐ VISA   ☐ MasterCard   ☐ DISCOVER

ACCOUNT #: _____

EXPIRATION DATE: _____

SIGNATURE: _____

Mail this page along with $2.00 shipping and handling to:
Historical Romance Book Club
PO Box 6640
Wayne, PA 19087
Or fax (must include credit card information) to:
610-995-9274
You can also sign up online at **www.dorchesterpub.com**.
*Plus $2.00 for shipping. Offer open to residents of the U.S. and Canada only.
Canadian residents please call 1-800-481-9191 for pricing information.
If under 18, a parent or guardian must sign. Terms, prices and conditions subject to change. Subscription subject to acceptance. Dorchester Publishing reserves the right to reject any order or cancel any subscription.